Praise for *Cross My Heart,*
THE HIDDEN DIARY, book 1

Cross My Heart was *very* descriptive (but not, like, overloaded!) and fun. It's a touching story that a lot of girls can relate to because of their own busy parents. I liked the mystery, too!

> Lilly, eleven years old, daughter of Liz Curtis Higgs,
> author of *Bad Girls of the Bible*

Mama mia! *Cross My Heart* was a great book! I liked the way the author left you hanging at the end of each chapter. It made you want to keep reading. I could really relate to some of the characters, and Claudette made me laugh. You'll love this book! Cross my heart!

> Tavia, ten years old, daughter of Deborah Raney,
> author of *A Vow to Cherish* and *Beneath a Southern Sky*

This book was really good, interesting, and fun. I couldn't say I had one favorite part because I loved the whole book! I couldn't put it down.

> Tyler, eleven years old, daughter of Lisa E. Samson,
> author of *The Church Ladies*

I couldn't put this book down! I guarantee you'll love *Cross My Heart,* and it will keep you on the edge of your seat.

> Marie, thirteen years old, daughter of Terri Blackstock,
> author of the NEWPOINTE 911 series

Cross My Heart is a very exciting book. Lucy . . . meets new friends and learns about God. I know my friends will love this book like I did. Maybe we'll find a hidden diary somewhere, too.

> Madelyn, nine years old, daughter of Cindy McCormick
> Martinusen, author of *Winter Passing*

I think Lucy and Serena are really cool. I can't wait to read the next HIDDEN DIARY book.

> Bethany, nine years old, daughter of Janet Holm McHenry,
> author of *PrayerWalk* and *Girlfriend Gatherings*

Books by
Sandra Byrd
FROM BETHANY HOUSE PUBLISHERS

THE
HIDDEN
DIARY

One Plus One

SANDRA BYRD

BETHANYHOUSE
MINNEAPOLIS, MINNESOTA

Published by Bethany House Publishers
A Ministry of Bethany Fellowship International
11400 Hampshire Avenue South
Bloomington, Minnesota 55438
www.bethanyhouse.com

Printed in the United States of America by
Bethany Press International, Bloomington, Minnesota 55438

Library of Congress Cataloging-in-Publication Data

Byrd, Sandra.
    One plus one / by Sandra Byrd.
        p.   cm. — (The hidden diary ; bk. 8)
Summary: When her friends on Catalina Island prepare for the annual tandem bicycle ride, Lucy finds herself wishing more than ever for a sister of her own.
ISBN 0-7642-2487-5 (pbk.)
    [1. Friendship—Fiction. 2. Bicycles and bicycling—Fiction.
3. Sisters—Fiction. 4. Christian life—Fiction. 5. Santa Catalina Island (Calif.)—Fiction.] I. Title. II. Series: Byrd, Sandra. Hidden diary ; bk. 8.
    PZ7.B9898   On   2002
    [Fic]—dc21   2002009661

To Natasha Sperling
I'm blessed to have you as
my HIDDEN DIARY *duet partner.*

Contents

Un-expectations

Late Saturday morning . . . D Day minus six

"Come on, girl!" Lucy leashed up her new puppy, then rubbed the dog behind her silky peach ears. Venus licked Lucy's hand in joy and thanks.

"If I give you lots of attention," Lucy whispered, "you won't be lonely for your mother and all your brothers and sisters." She patted Venus's head once more and headed toward the door.

"I'm going to the beach to read the diary with Serena," Lucy called to her mom, who was busily painting in the living room. Lucy slipped on her flower-powers and tossed her two-way radio into her beach bag. Then she slid her shades over her eyes and tied a Hawaiian-print bandanna loosely around Venus's neck. "Back in a couple of hours."

Mom nodded her agreement and blew her a kiss.

The street was hot and steamy, but wisps of cool breeze trailed through the air like kite tails. The sky was bright, like happiness.

9

On a day like this, what can possibly go wrong?

Each Saturday Lucy and her best friend, Serena, opened the Hidden Diary. At the beginning of the summer, the girls had found the diary, written in 1932 by Serena's great-grandmother and her best friend, Mary. Every week Lucy and Serena read a section of the old diary and did something just like the long-ago girls had done or seen or heard about. No matter what.

As soon as she arrived at the beach, Lucy spied Serena's yellow-and-white striped beach umbrella. Serena lazed underneath on a towel, her brown skin almost bronze with the summer sun. Lucy sniffed—coconut tanning oil and rotting seaweed, otherwise known as California sweet and sour.

Venus tugged against her leash, wanting to race to the water. Lucy scooped the pup into her arms instead.

When they got close, Serena heard them and sat up. "Oooh!" she squealed. "Venus is home!"

Lucy sat down next to her friend and smiled. "Yeah. She came home today."

"She looks very *cute* in her bandanna," Serena teased.

"You would know," Lucy said. "You're the Queen of *Cute*." She nodded at Serena's new hair clips, which matched her beach pullover perfectly.

"And you're the Queen of Ideas," Serena said. "What'cha got planned for us?"

"The diary, of course!" Lucy pulled the old red leather diary from her beach bag. Venus sat quietly on the beach—with the bribe of a teriyaki rawhide chew.

Serena scooted closer. "Open it up and let the adventure begin!"

Lucy cracked the cover and opened it up to that week's section. She handed it to Serena, who read the first section. It was written in the blocky handwriting of Serena's great-grandmother, also named Serena.

"Dear Diary,
Another week of fun and adventure. Can two girls take much more this summer?"

Serena held the book so Lucy could read aloud the next three words, written in feisty Mary's curly handwriting.

"YES! We can!"

Lucy grinned and let Serena take over.

"Well, we've had a shipwreck, we think. Not exactly us, actually, but near Catalina Island The lighthouse got some SOS—save our ship—messages overnight, and then suddenly they disappeared. Mitchell's dad was working last night, and mitchell spilled the beans to the whole crowd."

Lucy took over where Mary's writing began.

"So Serena and I are going to sneak down to the docks today, hang around, and see what's happening. Surely someone will fill us in! Who sent the messages for help? Did they get the help they needed? Or are they . . . gone? Stay tuned, dear Listener."

" 'Check back soon, Diary,' " Serena read the closing section.

"Hopefully I won't need to send an SOS to get us out of whatever pickle mary will surely get us into. Till then, Diary, ta-ta.
mary and Serena,
Faithful Friends."

Lucy snapped the diary shut. It startled Venus, who jumped. Lucy petted her back and said, "So what shall we do?"

"Wreck a ship?" Serena teased. "Find a friend named Mitchell?"

"Ha-ha!" The Idea Queen closed her eyes slightly, then opened them at once. "I know! Let's send an SOS!"

"We could get in *big* trouble for that."

"No, no, silly. Not a real one to the Coast Guard. Let's send out a signal for help—like send a letter or make a call for whatever kind of help we really need. And see if by the end of the week at D Day we've each had an answer. We'll keep it a secret from each other till then. It will be fun to share on Friday what the SOS was—and if our 'ship' was actually saved . . . or sank!"

Serena nodded. "But it has to be something we *really* need help with. Okay?"

Lucy agreed, and as she did, she heard footsteps, lots of them, on the sand behind her. She quietly slipped their private diary into Serena's beach bag, which was closest.

"Hi, guys!" Erica called out. She knelt down on the sand next to Venus. Venus rolled over on her back for a belly scratch, which Erica happily provided.

Right behind Erica was Amy, Erica's best friend, and Jenny, who had called Lucy last night to thank her for the turquoise ring Lucy had sent her a couple of weeks ago.

Lucy sneaked a look and noticed that Jenny had it on now. Jenny grinned and held her hand out for Lucy to see. Lucy winked back at her. Behind Jenny stood Julie and Betsy. Julie didn't exactly pat Lucy on the back, but at least she wasn't picking a fight.

Lucy looked them over. Everyone wore a powder blue T-shirt with bike wheels stitched all over it. In the middle were the words *One Plus One*.

"Hey, what's up with the matching T-shirts?" Lucy asked. "Are you a tribe now?"

Jenny laughed. "No, we all signed up for the bike rally this Friday. Everyone who signs up gets a T-shirt, every year." Jenny turned to Serena. "Did you sign up?"

"Roberto is signing us up today," Serena said. "Now that he's working at OutSpoken, he knows everything about bikes. Or so he thinks."

"Hey, I think I heard my dad talking about this!" Lucy said. She loved biking—and what could be more fun than biking with your friends? *All* of them? "He said the university sponsors a booth every year at the rally, handing out water bottles. Since he's on Catalina Island this summer, my parents have to be the ones to hand out the water bottles."

Lucy's dad and one other professor were spending the summer with their families on Catalina Island, twenty-six miles off the California coast, studying native plants for the university. For Lucy every summer was a summer away from her home in Seattle, but none had been as great as this one. She glanced at Serena, her best buddy, and smiled.

"Yes, that's right," Jenny chimed in. "There are lots of stops—water bottles, and ice cream, too!"

"And you get a groovy flag for your bike and stickers for your helmet. And we have pedal parties and a pancake breakfast to start it all off," Erica said.

Cool. Totally cool.

"It's a tandem ride," Amy spoke up, her voice trailing off. She blushed a little, not looking Lucy in the eye.

Weird. Since when is Amy shy with me?

Lucy looked right at the T-shirts. Yes, she could see now that the bikes on them were tandems, bicycles built for two. *Great!* Lucy thought she'd seen one stashed in the back of her dad's office.

"Even better! I've been wanting to ride one since I've been here. I just haven't had the time," Lucy said. Venus tugged at her leash a little; Lucy fed her a cheese cube to keep her calm.

"So are you going to ride in the One Plus One?" Julie asked.

Erica kicked the sand; Amy adjusted her sunglasses,

while Jenny got busy looking in a beach bag. No one looked up.

"Sure," Lucy said. "But only if Serena will be my partner," she joked, knowing full well Serena would ride with her.

Instead, unbelievably, Serena shook her head no. Lucy opened her mouth but said nothing.

A faint pink surfaced beneath Serena's bronze cheeks.

"I'm sorry," Serena said. "I can't be your partner."

A Secret SOS

Saturday afternoon . . .

The squawking sea gull gawking overhead made the only noise in their little corner of the beach. Lucy sat with her mouth open, Serena with her head down.

"Oh," Lucy finally said.

"It's not anything about you," Serena said. "It's just that . . . well, this tandem bike rally is kind of a brother-sister ride for us. We always ride together; we always have since it started four years ago, even when I could barely stay on the bike. We all ride with our brothers or sisters."

Lucy looked at the small circle of other girls sitting or standing nearby. Julie had a brother. Betsy had a sister. Both Amy and Erica had brothers and sisters. Then she looked at Jenny. Hey! She'd never seen a brother or sister with Jenny.

Jenny met Lucy's gaze and twisted the turquoise ring once before answering the unspoken question. "My step-brother is coming over from Los Angeles," she said quietly.

"Oh," Lucy said. Venus was tugging at the leash, and cheese cubes wouldn't quiet her down this time. Lucy stood up and brushed sand off of her freckly, too-white legs. As she did she caught Julie's eye. Julie was looking at Lucy with . . . well, pity.

Lucy's back stiffened. Why should *Julie*, of all people, feel sorry for her? She didn't need Julie's pity!

"It's a lot of fun," Amy said. "I wish you could come."

Everyone nodded their agreement.

"I think old Mr. Jaspers rides alone," Julie said. "Ever since his sister died."

"Not even Mr. Jaspers. His son rides with him now." Amy giggled. "In his navy blue dress socks and sailor shorts."

"I can't remember seeing anyone alone," Erica said. Then she looked at Lucy. "Oh."

Venus, meanwhile, wanted a swim. She tugged at the leash again.

Lucy laughed, though it felt a bit rough in her throat, more like a cough. "It's no problem. I'd better get this dog home before she races into the water and I have a wet pup!"

Everyone laughed, but the laughter stopped too soon to be real.

"I'll come," Serena said. "I was going home soon anyway."

Lucy shook her head. "No, stay here and have fun. Claudette's family is coming over. They're back from China."

"Claudette's dad works with Lucy's dad," Serena

explained to the others. "They just adopted a baby from China."

"How fun!" Amy said. Then it grew quiet again.

"I'll call you later," Lucy said to Serena. "Maybe tomorrow."

Serena nodded, her coffee-colored eyes brimming with compassion.

Lucy slipped on her sandals and headed toward the street.

"At least you have a cute dog!" someone called after her.

Lucy smiled. "Maybe I can get her on the back of the bike. What do you think?"

At that, the others laughed and turned back to their conversation.

"At least I have a dog," she said to herself, walking away. She looked down at Venus wagging her little tail.

Lucy stooped to rub Venus's shaggy neck. "No offense, girl. You know I love you. But . . . you're not really a brother or a sister. You know?"

Venus licked her hand again, and they kept walking, passing the villagers on the way. A lot of them wore powder blue T-shirts with bike wheels on them.

Riding a bicycle built for two would be fun. Those stops would all be fun, too—getting the groovy bike flags, the pancake breakfast with everyone. *I wish I could go.*

Oh well. I should be used to that *by now.* She remembered years ago when her next-door neighbor got a new baby brother. Lucy dressed up her dog, Jupiter, in a bonnet and booties and pushed him around in a stroller since she had no brother herself. And of course she was always doing things with just her parents almost every summer. Or with Claudette, who was much younger.

Speaking of Claudette, her family's golf cart was parked in front of Lucy's house. No one on Catalina regularly drove cars in the tiny tourist town, only golf carts. And bicycles. Lucy tied Venus to a shady spot in the backyard, gave her some fresh water, and walked to the cottage to let Venus nap.

If Claudette was there, the new baby would be, too. Lucy slipped off her sandals and walked in the house.

"I'm back!" She stepped into the kitchen, where everyone was gathered.

"You're home early." Mom reached for Lucy with her one open arm. In the other arm rested the new baby.

Lucy replied to her mother but kept looking at the baby—her big brown eyes and soft chubby cheeks. "Yeah. Everyone was going on and on about some brother-sister or sister-sister bike ride."

"Hi, Lucy!" Claudette came racing from the other half of the room, her hair flying behind her. "Let me introduce you!"

Lucy's mother kissed the baby on the cheek. "Are there *any* more cuties where you came from, precious?" She kissed her other cheek and then handed the little girl over to Claudette.

"We shouldn't hold my sister too close," Claudette said. "The social worker said if I hold her too close it could squeeze her."

Lucy could see her mother hold back a smile.

Claudette took the baby and brought her close to Lucy.

"She's fifteen months old," Claudette said. "That's almost a year and a half. Her name is Chantal."

Lucy reached her hand toward Chantal. The baby caught it and giggled. Her whole face smiled, and her little pigtails shook on each side of her head, like two calligraphy brushes, soft and black, being shaken dry.

Oh, does Claudette know how thankful she should be? Lucy would be *really* thankful if this baby, or one like her, were *Lucy's* sister.

"She's adorable. Can I hold her?"

Claudette's brows knitted. "I guess so. The rule is, though, we're not supposed to pass her around too much."

Claudette's mom spoke up. "Yes, but actually, it's great that Lucy is home early. I was hoping maybe she could baby-sit Chantal for an hour or two while we go to pick up your puppy, Claudette. Just the three of us. Once we get the puppy situated, we'll come back and get the baby."

Claudette spun to face her mother. "My puppy gets to come home today, too. Yippee!"

Then she looked doubtful. "Will Lucy be okay with Chantal, though?"

Lucy rolled her eyes but smiled. "I do just fine baby-sitting you, Claudette!"

Mrs. Kingsley said, "I thought ahead a little and brought over what you'd need just in case. I'm sure Lucy can handle things smoothly if anything comes up. And Chantal has been so pleasant and happy with everyone!"

"I'll be here, too," Lucy's mother said. "But if you've got everything planned out, Lucy'll be fine. Life is like a painting—when you carefully plan things, the final picture always ends up looking good! And you always plan things out so well, Grace."

Did Mom have to make *everything* relate to painting? Lucy grinned to herself. But Mom *had* said, "Lucy'll be fine." Good old Mom.

So Mrs. Kingsley left Chantal's things on the counter top, and the three of them headed off. "But, Mom, didn't the social worker say not to separate the baby from her family for a month or two?" Claudette asked, her voice trailing off as they walked outside.

Lucy shut the door behind them.

"Okay." Lucy picked up Chantal. *Please don't cry,* she thought. Then she whispered it aloud to the baby. "Please don't cry."

After checking to make sure that Lucy was okay and giving the baby another smooch, Lucy's mom went back to painting. "Call me if you need me, honey," she said as she left the room.

Lucy peeked out the kitchen window at Venus, still snoozing under the tree. All that running around had tired her out.

She looked at Chantal. Chantal smiled. Lucy smiled back.

It was going to be okay.

First Lucy sat down on the floor with her and grabbed the string of balloons that Dad had blown up last night as a "Welcome Home" for Chantal that morning. They didn't have helium, so the balloons were getting kind of soggy.

Lucy bopped one, and it bounced toward the baby. The baby looked startled and then giggled.

Lucy bopped another one, and it popped.

Chantal began to cry. "Oh no! Please don't cry." Lucy grabbed the popped pink balloon, which lay on the floor like a piece of chewed gum. Then she threw it away. Even she knew that getting ahold of that could choke Chantal.

Should have thought it out in advance instead of just playing with the first thing I came across.

Lucy picked the baby up and walked away from the remaining soggy balloon, over toward the kitchen table. As she brushed against it, some newspapers fell on the floor.

"Mama mia!" Lucy said.

Chantal stopped crying and started laughing. Lucy knocked another piece of newspaper onto the floor. "Mama mia!" she said again, and Chantal giggled. For the next five minutes Lucy knocked piece after piece of paper onto the floor, and Chantal laughed. That laugh, that smile—Lucy was hooked.

"You are just full of cute juice," Lucy said. The baby's pigtails swished, and her little fist bopped Lucy on the cheek.

"Want a drink?" Lucy asked.

As she walked over to the counter, she scanned the items Mrs. Kingsley had left. *Sippy cup, toys, diapers.* And a manila envelope labeled *Helpful Information.*

On the front of the envelope there was the name of the adoption agency, and stapled next to it was the business card of the social worker.

While Chantal sipped her water, Lucy looked at the card. It said *Miriam Chin. Helping dreams come true for families around the world. Please call, write, or email.* Then it gave a phone number, street address, and email address.

Lucy looked toward the door, where her beach bag still sat from her morning with Serena. *I wish Mrs. Chin could help my dreams come true.*

She looked out the window and saw a tandem ride by—sisters, laughing together. Just like Claudette and Chantal would be soon.

Lucy closed her eyes. She needed a sister or a brother. One or the other. Not just for the bike race, as much as she wished she could go. It wasn't just about the bike race. It was about year after year of being alone so much.

But what would her parents say?

Well, what *had* Mom just told Mrs. Kingsley? *"When you carefully plan things, the final picture always ends up looking good!"*

If Lucy planned it well—prepared well for it, got all the information lined up, and asked them at just the right time—they'd know she wasn't rushing, that she was serious. That this might be a new idea—but that the need was real. So she'd do it right.

Suddenly Lucy knew just whom to send an SOS to for her Diary Deed. This was a real need; nobody could deny that. And she certainly needed help.

Lucy took Chantal out of the kitchen and took the manila envelope with her, too. Her mom was busy, and Dad was nowhere in sight. Napping, probably. As was Venus.

Lucy went into the computer nook, Chantal on her lap, and logged on to their email.

Dear Mrs. Chin, she started typing. *I am very interested in getting your adoption packet right away.* Lucy gave their Catalina post-office box number and then signed the email, *Sincerely, Lucy Larson.*

She held her breath and clicked Send.

The message was sent.

Lucy looked at Chantal and smiled. Chantal hit her again, softly, with her chubby fist and smiled back. "You are just too cute," Lucy said, kissing the baby's powdery-soft cheek.

Lucy closed down the computer. Soon the packet would arrive. And then Lucy would look it over, get all the facts lined up, and present her idea at just the right time.

It was important that she get it all planned out well and have it prepared for just the right moment. She'd look through the papers and be ready with great answers for anything they might object to. She'd start helping out more, too, so they would see it wouldn't be too much trouble.

But . . . it was important that no one find out till she was completely ready to present her case.

Choices

Sunday . . . D Day minus five

Lucy had set her alarm clock to 7:29, but she woke up even earlier to the sound of crying.

Whimpering, actually. She'd heard it during the night, too, just a little. Venus was crying for her mother and the fuzzy brothers and sisters she was used to snuggling up with at night.

Lucy tiptoed toward the stairs but then heard whistling and realized that her parents were already awake.

"We'll be down in a minute," Dad called out. She heard the shower go on and knew that her mom was getting ready for church.

Lucy hurried to the living room and opened the door to Venus's crate. The dog rushed out at her and licked Lucy's face.

Lucy laughed. *Dog kisses. Nothin' else like 'em.*

Lucy passed the computer on her way to take Venus to the backyard. It was shut off, and she probably wouldn't have time to turn it on before going to church.

I wonder if Mrs. Chin got my email and is preparing the adoption packet today.

Venus ran back into the laundry room from outside and wrestled with a bath towel. Lucy stirred warm water into the dry dog food.

"You're still a baby, after all," she whispered. "Let's make it soft for you."

Venus nuzzled Lucy, then went back to eat.

Lucy went into the kitchen. *Hey! I'll make some coffee for Mom and Dad. When they see what a huge help I can be to them, they won't worry that a baby will be so much work.*

She got the grinder and the beans out, then filled the grinder up to the brim with beans and plugged it in. She let the grinder run a long, long time. Then she poured the grinds into a filter, nearly filling it, and slid it into the coffeepot.

Venus came in, her little tail wagging out an even beat, like Lucy's piano metronome.

"Wanna watch, girl?" *Now, how much water?* They each drank about two cups in the morning, so Lucy filled to the four-cup water line.

She turned the button to On and headed upstairs to get dressed. Venus ran along behind, though she wasn't so sure of the stairs at first.

Lucy slipped into a pair of pressed khakis and a T-shirt with a glittering heart on it. Venus fought with a box of Kleenex. After Venus had shredded several, barking at the pieces as they floated away on the wood floor, Lucy took the box away from her.

"You silly dog," she said. "Training for you this afternoon."

Once downstairs she saw her mother transferring her coffee from a small cup into an especially large mug.

"Hi!" Lucy said.

"Good morning." Her mom poured milk into her coffee—a lot of milk.

"All that milk in your coffee? I thought you liked it with just sugar."

"Not today," her mom said. "I'm, uh, trying to get more calcium."

Lucy couldn't be sure, but it looked like her mom grimaced as she swallowed some coffee and quickly set the mug by the side of the sink.

"I hope it's okay that I made it," Lucy said. "I'm trying to be helpful."

"I know you are," her mom answered. "I appreciate how mature you're getting."

Lucy smiled as she slipped her shoes on. If she were more mature, a baby wouldn't be too much work for anyone. Right?

It was almost time for church, so they put Venus into her crate. Lucy tossed in a squeaky ball and a teriyaki rawhide. Venus still whined and cried, though, not used to being alone.

Please don't let her cry the whole morning away, Lord. Lucy promised herself she wouldn't be too distracted at church thinking about Venus.

Ring ding! a bell chimed as someone biked past the Larsons on their way to church. A tandem bike. *Ring ding!*

A brother in back and a sister in front, it looked like. They laughed together in the special way that brothers and sisters do, teasing. "Keep going. I don't want to do all the work," the sister called back.

Her brother grinned and tweaked her ponytail, poking out from underneath her helmet.

Lucy focused on walking up the stairs to church.

An older man met them at the door, someone Lucy didn't know. Jake wasn't handing out bulletins today. Oh well. Her sparkly shirt looked nice anyway.

Lucy's parents headed in to sit next to Claudette's family, in the same pew. Lucy sat next to Claudette, who sat next to her mother, who held Chantal on her lap.

Chantal grinned her four-tooth smile—two on top, two on bottom—in Lucy's direction. Lucy beamed back.

Claudette leaned over and squeezed Lucy's hand. "Hi. How's the dog?"

"Good," Lucy said. "How about yours?"

"Okay, but he cried last night," Claudette said. "Between Duke and Chantal, someone is crying all the time."

Chantal looked pretty happy now, though. Cute. Her little arm rested on Claudette's arm. She must already know that she and Claudette would be special to one another. Sisters.

The piano player, a middle-aged woman that Lucy hadn't seen before, stopped just then. She sure played well, though, and even played cool new songs. Lucy knew good piano. She looked the woman in the eye and smiled appreciatively.

"Good morning!" the pastor welcomed them. "We have a baby dedication today. As a small church, we tend to just dedicate them when they come. Today the Kingsleys come with their new daughter, Chantal Lian."

At that, Claudette's whole family moved forward to the front of the church. "This wonderful family has given a home to a little girl. They've just brought her back from China. The Bible tells us that God is the father to the fatherless, but also that we are our brothers' keepers and need to love and care for one another. While God will remain an important part of this little girl's life, she also has a new father and mother and sister to love her. And she will be a blessing to them, too. Psalm sixty-eight, verses five and six, tells us that God takes care of widows and orphans and sets the lonely in families."

Claudette beamed and pulled the baby's dress a little to neaten some wrinkles.

Lucy closed her eyes. *Lonely.* The word really stuck out.

After the baby was dedicated, the Kingsleys came back to their seat. Lucy listened to the sermon, also looking around for some of her friends. Erica was there with her family. Jake wasn't. Where was he? Lucy sort of looked forward to seeing him each week at least once. She looked down at her fingernails, painted to match her sparkly shirt.

All of a sudden a beeping noise went off next to Lucy. What was that?

She looked at Claudette, who looked down at her watch. *Mama mia!* Claudette must have set the alarm on her watch, and now it was ringing! The pastor stopped talking, and the *whole church* looked back at their pew.

Claudette, not upset at all, finally shut the alarm off. "Time to feed Chantal," she whispered to her mother. "It's been four hours."

Most people turned back around to face the front again.

"Chantal is fine." Her mother's whisper sounded more like ice than feathers.

"It *can't* wait," Claudette said. "The social worker said every four hours, especially at first."

Mrs. Kingsley's lips drew tight like a purse string. "It was a guideline, Claudette, not a rule."

The pastor went on speaking, and when they stood to sing the final song, Claudette looked over at Lucy and spoke to her for the first time since they had sat down again.

"It was a rule," she said firmly. Lucy was glad Jake wasn't there today after all.

On the way home, several other tandems whizzed by.

Lucy spent the afternoon playing piano and playing catch with Venus. Serena was riding bikes with Roberto and having a picnic with her family today.

"I'm glad to see how much responsibility you're taking with Venus," Mom said, running her fingers through Lucy's hair and smiling.

Lucy grinned, too. She had also cleaned up the lunch dishes.

🌂 🌂 🌂

Later that night, when her dad was *still* on the

computer, Lucy began to wonder if she'd ever get a chance to check her email. She didn't want to ask and prompt questions, though.

"Why's he on there so long?" she asked. Venus snoozed in her crate.

"He's working ahead since he'll miss some time when we work the One Plus One booth this week," her mom said. "Would you like to work the water bottle table with us? I hadn't even asked."

Just then her dad came in. Lucy was glad she hadn't really had to answer her mom's question—yet. They all sat at the kitchen table to eat. After praying, Lucy picked at her pizza.

"I thought you liked pizza," Dad said.

"It's kind of boring."

Finally Lucy blurted out, "I've always wanted to ride a two-person bike. And all of my friends are riding. I don't want to be stuck with the grown-ups again." *Dumb old only-child syndrome. Doing stuff with grown-ups night and day.*

"Why not ride, then?" her dad said.

Lucy rolled her eyes. "With who?"

"Don't roll your eyes, Lucy," her mother answered. "I'll go with you."

"It's for siblings," Lucy said. "You know, brothers and sisters."

"I know what siblings are," her dad answered. "Who said it was for siblings?"

"My friends." Lucy peeled the cheese back off her pizza like stripping off a layer of skin. "You know, the ones who live here all the time. I think *they* should know." She rolled her eyes again. She wished she hadn't, but she didn't stop herself. A scar she'd thought had healed in her heart, that of having no sibling, oozed again from somewhere deep inside.

"We can have this conversation without you being unpleasant. Maybe you should go to your room until you can talk with more respect," Dad said.

Holding back tears, Lucy excused herself. On the way she grabbed the lone balloon left over from Chantal's visit and took it with her.

It bobbed along as she carried it, but the farther she walked, the droopier it became.

Once in her room, she sat on her bed with the soggy balloon on her lap. Then she drew Tender Teddy into her lap. Then the Woodstock she and Serena had bought at Knott's Berry Farm.

"I need some help, God." She closed her eyes. "I'm not my normal self. I don't know what to do. I'm lonely, and I wish I had a sister. Or even a brother, if he wasn't a pest. Please talk to me, God."

Lucy turned on a CD, hoping the words would say something meaningful, something she'd know was a message from God. The music was good, but she didn't get any message.

She opened up her Bible. "I'll just let it fall open, and maybe God will be telling me something right there!"

She started reading. It was about someone named Elijah stopping the rain. Good story, lots of faith. Didn't have anything to do with being an *only*.

A knock came at the door. "May I come in?" her mother asked.

"Sure."

Mom walked in and sat on the bed next to Lucy. "I'm sorry about the ride."

"And I'm sorry about the way I spoke to you and Dad. Will you forgive me? I'll ask Daddy, too."

Mom nodded and hugged Lucy. "You and I could go to Los Angeles on Thursday night, stay until Saturday. We could go shopping and have a good time there. When we come back, this whole thing will have blown over. Dad could probably handle the university's water booth with the Kingsleys."

Lucy thought about it. It *would* be fun. Just her and her mom. No worries about brothers and sisters, not having to watch everyone else or hide out in her house during the whole thing like a criminal.

But . . . even if she couldn't ride, she really didn't want to miss the whole rally—the flags and stickers and the pancake breakfast.

Lucy heard Venus bark downstairs. Besides, what about Venus? Dad would be home . . . but only sometimes.

"Or else," her mom said, "you might want to check into how you could ride after all."

"How's that?" Lucy asked.

"I don't know," her mom said. "But you are the Idea Queen, right?"

Lucy allowed a little smile to escape.

"I'm going to let Venus out," Mom said. "Let me know what you decide."

Idea Queen. Hmm. The very words gave Lucy an idea. She picked up the phone and dialed.

A Terrible Mix-up

"Well, did you call the One Plus One organizer lady?" Serena opened the door to her house and slipped outside onto the porch.

"I did." Lucy smiled. "But I had to leave a message because no one was home. I'm hoping she'll call early and let me know if it's okay." Lucy pointed to the two-way radio clipped to her jean shorts. "My mom said she'd radio over if I got a phone call."

Serena smiled. "Okay. Then let's go and clean up the bike."

They went around to the back of Serena's house to the small shed where they kept their mower, garden tools, and bikes. The big tandem was in there, but so was Serena's single bike, parked next to it.

Even if they said it was okay, the single bike seemed kind of small and . . . well, *single*, next to the tandem bike. It brought home what was going to happen here. If Lucy rode the single bike, she might feel weird next to all those brothers and sisters on a tandem. It might look strange, too. But if she just stood at the booth with her parents, she'd have to paint on a fakey smile when everyone was riding by. And she'd miss all the fun.

She could go to L.A. with her mom and skip the whole deal. As much fun as the bike rally sounded, going to L.A. was starting to sound okay, too.

"It looks pretty clean," Serena said. "Do you want to bring it home today?"

"Nah." Lucy shook her head. "I can't ride a bike with little muttsters here." She patted Venus on the head. "But thanks for letting me borrow it—maybe. I'll let you know when she calls."

"Okay."

Venus ran around Serena's legs in circles, getting her leash all wound up. Serena giggled. "I wish I had a dog. My old cat is snuggly, but she doesn't like to play."

"Want to share Venus for the summer?" Lucy offered. "We could train her together. It would be a lot of fun."

Serena smiled. "Yeah, I would. Are you sure it's okay?"

"Of course! As far as I'm concerned, she can be *our* dog. She just has to sleep at my house, because of your dad's allergies. If you help train her, she'll grow close to you, too."

"Really? Where should we start?"

Lucy pulled out a plastic pack of treats. "She'll do anything for these." Lucy popped one into her own mouth. Serena looked at her, horrified.

"LUCY! You're eating dog treats!"

Lucy laughed and passed the bag to Serena. "Don't worry, they're peanut butter puff cereal. Try one."

Serena popped one into her own mouth. "Yum."

When Venus saw the bag, she immediately sat down and looked up at the girls expectantly.

"See? She knows what they are." Lucy generously handed the leash over to her friend. "Why don't you work on 'Come' with her." Lucy showed Serena how to train the dog and gave Serena the bag of puffs.

Lucy sat on the grass and tried, unsuccessfully, to weave a daisy chain while Serena and Venus, unleashed now, ran around the backyard. After half an hour, both of them were tired. The girls lay in the grass, chatting, while Venus enjoyed a tummy scratch.

Suddenly a voice crackled over the radio. "Lucy?"

It was her mom.

"Yes?"

"There's a phone message for you here. Want to come home and return the call?"

"Be right home, Mom."

Lucy leashed up Venus and said good-bye to Serena. "I'll call you later and let you know what she says, okay?"

"Okay," Serena answered. Lucy was nearly out of the backyard when she thought of something and hurried back toward her friend. Serena looked puzzled as Lucy walked back toward her.

"Let's pray," Lucy said quietly. "Just that this will work out, okay?"

"Of course." Serena held on to Lucy's hand while Lucy prayed that the whole situation would work out, that Lucy would be able to ride and not feel silly about it. Serena prayed, too.

Feeling better now, certain that the day would flow the way she wanted it to, Lucy and Venus ran down Marine Way, around the corner, and down to 234 Pebble Road, where Lucy's summer cottage was located.

She put the dog in her crate for a little snooze. Puppies, like babies, needed a lot of sleep.

"I'm going back to paint," her mother said, pushing her blond hair behind her ears. "Unless it's an emergency, please don't disturb me. I'm feeling a little rushed. Barbara called today and said the client needs to have this by Tuesday, which means I've got to have this ready by Friday night so it can dry. It's nowhere near done. After it's done, I'll have much more free time. Okay, honey?"

Lucy nodded and kissed her mom's cheek, then raced into the kitchen to the phone. Her mom had written the phone number and name on a sticky yellow paper and then attached it to the phone.

Lucy dialed.

"Hello?" came a voice on the other end.

"Yes, this is Lucy Larson, returning your call."

"Hello, Lucy. What can I help you with?"

"I was wondering, since I know you're the organizer of the One Plus One race this weekend, would it be okay if I rode a single bike instead of a tandem?"

The quiet air stood between them. Finally the answer came.

"I'm sorry, Lucy, but this is a tandem rally. Part of the rules for this, and what makes it so much fun, is that only tandems ride. We do have several other bike rallies planned for the summer in which you could ride a single bike. Can I send you a brochure on them?"

Lucy squeezed her ten-gallon sorrow back into her one-gallon heart. "No, thank you. It's just that, well, I don't have a sibling."

"Oh my," the woman responded. "You don't have to ride with a sibling! You can ride with a cousin or a parent or a friend."

"Thank you for the idea," Lucy said. "Good-bye."

She quietly set the phone down and looked out the back window. Serena's yard was kitty-corner from her own.

A friend doesn't work if all of your friends have siblings.

Lucy sighed and walked toward the living room, but her mom had already closed the door and was painting. Normally her mom only closed the door when she was stressed.

Lucy headed toward her room.

Wait! She had been so wrapped up in the phone call that she hadn't checked her email that morning.

Quickly she logged on.

She turned and looked over her shoulder while the computer came up. Not that she was doing anything wrong, but she just wanted it to be oh-so-right when she presented her case.

Yes! An email from a Mrs. Chin had arrived last night! Lucy opened the file and eagerly read.

Dear Mrs. Larson,

Uh-oh. Mrs. Larson?! *She thinks I'm my mother!*

Lucy kept reading.

I would be glad to personally deliver the adoption information packet to you on Catalina Island late this Friday afternoon. I happen to be making a visit to a new adoptive family in just a few days for their one-week follow-up. I can bring the packet by your house in person just before dinner. I'll look forward to meeting you then and getting you started on the road to adoption. I'll bring by my paper work, which should explain everything, and the outlines showing just how easy this can be for the right family.

Lucy nearly jumped off of her chair. *Oh no! Mrs. Chin must be coming to check on Claudette's family. And she thinks I'm my mother!*

But wait. Lucy breathed easy for a minute. She'd only given Mrs. Chin the P.O. Box number. Right? So how could she stop by?

Lucy checked her "sent" folder to scan the email she'd sent to Mrs. Chin.

Oh no. No, no, no. Yes, Lucy had only given her email address, but her dad had programmed the computer to attach a signature to each email sent from the computer. Along with *Larson Family*, it gave their phone number, all three email addresses, and the P.O. Box. And, because he often got packages overnighted to him for work, it said *234 Pebble Road.*

Mrs. Chin knew where they lived.

Lucy skipped back to Mrs. Chin's email.

I'll be out of the office on vacation till I arrive on

Catalina (which will seem like a vacation, too!), so you won't be able to reach me. If you won't be home on Friday, I'll just leave the packet on the doorstep and you can call with questions.
Sincerely,
Miriam Chin.

Lucy closed her eyes and began to sweat.
Mrs. Chin would be there on Friday.

An Idea

Tuesday evening . . . D Day minus three

"I've noticed you watching the tandem bikes, Lucy," Dad said the next night at dinner. "So I brought one home for you tonight. It was stored in the back room at the office. Someone must have used it during other summers on Catalina."

Lucy tried to smile. Her dad worked hard to make her happy, she knew. Her mom was in the living room painting again, so it was just the two of them.

"Thanks, Dad."

"Do you want to go for a ride with me before your mom and I go to the meeting at church tonight?"

Oh yeah. Their marriage class. Last year Lucy's parents had separated; this summer they were taking a marriage-builders class with other couples who had struggled but were committed to staying married.

"No, thanks. Maybe afterward, okay?" She didn't want to completely let him down after he'd tried so hard.

"Okay. We'll drop you off at Claudette's house on the way to church. Your mom is working right up to the second we leave. She's feeling a lot of pressure to get the work done—and done right—by Friday night so it has time to dry completely before she packs it off. A new client is buying this painting for a book cover."

"Okay. But, Dad? I don't really want to go to Claudette's tonight while you're at the class." Lucy pushed away half of her ham-and-cheese sandwich. *Boring.*

"Why not?"

Lucy folded her napkin into a little square, smaller and smaller till it was almost a ball. Then she crunched it into her fist. "I just don't, not tonight. Claudette keeps going on and on about her molars coming in late, and I'm not up to hearing about it, that's all."

"All right," her dad agreed. Lucy could tell by looking at his face that he understood what it was *really* about. "Why don't you bring a book and sit in the church and wait for us, okay?"

Lucy nodded. She cleared the table and stuffed the dishes into the dishwasher, then ran upstairs and changed into an old T-shirt. Just for fun, she decided to slip a pair of glitter clips into her strawberry-blond tangle of curls.

They took off in the golf cart, zooming down the street and around the corner, pulling up next to the sweet white-and-green church. The flowers Jake had planted around the church at the beginning of the summer had flourished and thrived, happily spreading like good news throughout all the grounds.

Oh, I forgot my book! Lucy thought as they parked their

cart on the street and headed up the stairs.

But when she walked in, she took a Bible from a stack near the door and settled down into a pew. *This is even better than my book,* she thought to herself, smiling. It hadn't always felt that way.

Best time spent reading is with the Book.

She opened it up. The pages still crackled with newness, and the gold was bright on the pages' edges; many fingers had not yet rubbed it off.

She closed her eyes and listened. From far away came the sound of the boats leaving the docks, and closer, golf carts rumbled up and down the street.

Jake's flowers had opened their petals, like tight fists unfolding their fingers, and the scent deep in their hearts escaped to perfume the air. Life was not perfect, but this moment came close.

Lucy turned to the section in Matthew that came next in her devotions. She drank in the words, for once actually just listening to what God had to say instead of begging for an answer to her questions or a solution to her problems. It felt good.

A middle-aged woman came from the door behind the altar and stepped to the piano. "Excuse me!" she said to Lucy. "I didn't know anyone else would be in here. I need to practice for next Sunday's service. Will that bother you?"

Lucy closed the Bible. "Not at all. I'm a piano player myself, so I'd love to listen to you. You played on Sunday, too, right?"

The woman nodded and came down the aisle. "My name is Mariette. I'm a friend of the pastor's family."

"My name is Lucy." Lucy stuck her hand out to shake Mariette's. "I'm just waiting for my parents; they're in the class downstairs."

"Nice to meet you." Mariette shook her hand.

Piano fingers, Lucy thought, noticing the long, lean fingers and the short nails. Mariette smiled warmly before walking back to the piano.

As Mariette played, Lucy closed her eyes and thought. She needed to tell her parents about the adoption packet, that was certain. She had planned to tell them all along, of course. And yet she didn't want to tell her parents *now* in a panic. They'd think she was just acting on an impulsive whim again, and perhaps that she wasn't as serious about this as she really, truly was. The moment needed to be just right.

Besides, her mom was in a total rush to get her painting done by Friday evening. This wouldn't be a good time to tell them. Lucy wanted her—actually, all of them—to be calm when considering this. Her mom had lots of time, usually; it was just these little bursts. When this little burst was over, she'd be ready to relax. She always was.

I have it! I'll plan a dinner for Friday night. And I'll do all the work—all the preparation and cleaning up. I'll present the whole packet to them then. I'll look it over first and see if there are any questions that I can help think up a solution for in advance. Mom will be relaxed. Her painting will be ready to go. I'll sit on the porch all afternoon to get the packet when it comes on Friday. Venus and I can hang out there, training and playing.

There'd be no trip to L.A. with her mother, or she'd

miss Mrs. Chin. She'd have to stay and face the One Plus One . . . somehow.

Lucy opened her eyes. She felt small and alone on the pew, no one on either side of her for a long way. She imagined tidying a little sister's dress. *It would be wonderful to have someone to share life with.*

Mariette finished her song and looked at Lucy. "So you're a piano player, eh? Want to come up and play a duet?"

"Oh no, I'm not as good as you are."

Mariette scooted over on the bench. "Come on. It's just the two of us."

Lucy smiled a bit and walked up front. No one else could hear, after all.

Mariette reached into her black tote bag and pulled out some music. "Can you play this?"

Lucy sat down next to Mariette and looked at the song. It was "A Midsummer Night's Dream for Piano Four Hands."

"Yes," she said.

"It is a midsummer night, after all." Mariette smiled and Lucy smiled back. The two of them played through the piece once, roughly, with just a few mistakes. Lucy laughed. "Can we play that again? No one else in my house plays the piano, so I don't get to play duets very often."

"Me neither," Mariette said. They played it again. The music was soft and light, like a dusky night, and dreamy, as promised.

Four hands are better than two, it seemed to Lucy. She sighed.

Then Mariette said, "I'd like to play something else for you."

She took out some music and played. Lucy closed her eyes and drank it in. *Wow.* "What was that?" she asked.

"I'm playing that for Wendy's wedding at the end of the summer," Mariette said. "Do you know Wendy?"

"Oh yes," Lucy said. "She worked at the camp I went to a couple of weeks ago. And she's Rachel's sister. I love Rachel."

Mariette nodded and smiled.

"Did you have that song at your wedding?" Lucy asked. "I can tell how much you love it."

Mariette closed the music. Quietly, she said, "I'm not married."

"Oh."

Mariette slipped her music back into the black tote. "I hope it might still happen, could still happen, but in the meantime, if it doesn't, it's okay. Though sometimes being at weddings is hard."

"But if it makes you sad, why do you still go to them and play piano?"

"I do it for my friends. I want to be there with them, to share the joy, to enjoy the wedding, to have fun at the reception with them. I've learned to lean on God to help me push the sad part away a little at a time so I don't miss the happy parts."

Lucy looked out the open door as two people raced by on a tandem bike. "I know what you mean."

"Maybe God still has someone planned for me. Who knows?"

Mariette played a jaunty little tune before closing the piano. She did it so well, with joy. Lucy smiled. *Sometimes two hands are okay, too.*

Mariette gathered up her music and said good-bye. Lucy checked her watch. There was still half an hour to go.

As she settled back into the pew and prepared to open the Bible again, she heard footsteps behind her. She turned around to look. *Jake!*

She smiled in spite of herself.

"Hey, Dr Pepper!" he said. "Long time no see!"

"Hey, Chief," she said. "I noticed you weren't in church on Sunday." *Oh no!* Now he'd know she'd been looking for him. Well, not really, but kind of.

"I was at my grandmother's for a few days," he said. "I just came by to see if my dad was here. He was going to do some painting in here this week. What are you doing?"

"Waiting for my parents," Lucy said. "They're in a class downstairs."

"Ah. Well, good seeing you. Are you going to ride in the One Plus One on Friday?"

Lucy fiddled with the glitter clip in her hair. "No. I don't have anyone to ride with. I don't have a brother or sister. Serena and the rest of my friends are riding with their brothers and sisters."

Jake sat down next to her in the pew. His face reflected real concern for her. "Well," he finally said, "maybe I have an idea."

An Unanswered Question

Wednesday . . . D Day minus two

The next morning Lucy woke up thinking about Jake's idea. It might work. First she'd have to see if Roberto could help with the bike. In her own mind Lucy had named the bike Fireball.

"Serena's going to be here in a couple of minutes," Lucy said. She and her mom were finishing a late breakfast. Dad had left early. "Is it okay if I spend the day with her?"

"Of course." Mom's face betrayed the tiniest corner of relief. "I've got a lot to do. Want to see the painting so far?"

Lucy scooped the last bit of soft-boiled egg out of its holder with a tiny golden spoon. "Yes!"

She followed her mom into the living room and saw her mom's canvas, about half done. "Lots of details take lots of time," her mom said. "And oils are harder for me. I am trying to be done before we go to Los Angeles so the painting will be dry in enough time to ship."

"Oh," Lucy said. "Well, I don't think we have to go to Los Angeles, if it's okay with you. I mean, I'd love to go with you, and we can go another time, you know, mother and daughter. But I kind of want to be home on Friday."

"For the One Plus One?" Her mother looked perplexed.

"Yes . . . and other things."

"Are you going to ride? I thought Dad said when the two of you got on the bike last night something was wrong with it."

"Roberto is going to see if he can fix it."

"Good!" The tension wrinkles melted away into the smooth skin on her mom's face. Lucy knew her mom was glad for the extra time to finish her work. And Lucy was glad she'd be home on Friday afternoon when Mrs. Chin would stop by.

Mom slipped her painting apron over her clothes. For once she looked just like a regular mom who cooked and baked. *Not!* Lucy giggled.

Before her mom closed the door to paint, Lucy decided to pop the big question. "Mom? Since we're not going to L.A. on Friday, I wondered if I could plan a special dinner for you and Dad on Friday night. Will you be done with your painting by then?"

"I certainly hope so, or I'm in big trouble. It needs to be completely dry by Monday. And that takes nearly three days. And I'd love a special dinner from my special girl."

Mom quickly kissed Lucy's cheek and then closed the

door. A few minutes later Lucy heard the classical music flip on and knew her mom would be oblivious to real life for a couple of hours.

She looked out the window. No Serena. She stepped into the laundry room and wheeled out the bright red bike that her dad had brought home from work last night. He and Lucy had tried to ride last night after church, in the dusk, but something was wrong with the bike. Lucy wheeled it out onto the porch, and Venus yipped at the wheels.

"You think the moving wheels are little animals, don't you, girl." Venus looked up at Lucy and barked, something she didn't do often. Lucy smiled. "You're my guard dog. Little big stuff."

As soon as she wheeled the bike outside, Lucy saw Serena walking toward her. Lucy waved. Serena waved back and sped down the street even faster.

"So this is it?" Serena said. She looked over the red-and-white tandem.

"This is it, all right. But I don't know if Roberto can fix it."

Serena smiled. "He probably can. He's pretty good. He won't be home till after lunch, though. Do you want to come to my house and hang out and wait? Then we can go to the beach afterward."

Serena knelt down to give Venus a hug, and Venus licked Serena's cheek.

Lucy smiled. "Do *you* want to put the leash on her?"

"Oh yes!" Serena said. The three of them traipsed into the house. Lucy scooped some peanut butter cereal balls into a bag, along with some cheese cubes, and got her plastic Jelly Belly container. Serena snapped the leash onto Venus's rhinestone-studded collar.

"Very cute collar."

"I figured if I can't be glamorous, my dog might as well be." Lucy slipped her sandals on. Then she opened the door to the living room. "I'm leaving. I'll be back later this afternoon."

"Got your radio?"

"Yes."

"Stay with Serena or come right home," her mom instructed. Lucy promised she would.

"Love you," her mom said.

"So," Serena said as they walked back up Pebble Road and toward the corner to turn to Serena's, "Jake thinks you should ride with Claudette, eh?"

"Yeah." Lucy walked the troubled tandem while Serena held Venus's leash. " 'That little pesty girl who's always tagging after you,' he called her."

"Did you think he was going to ask you to ride with him at first?"

Lucy felt her pink skin turn pinker. "Since you're my very best friend, I'll admit it, but only to you. Yes. But at least I didn't say anything to him about *that*!"

Serena laughed. "I know."

"He talked about his friend Philip. You know, *Philip*." Lucy winked at Serena. It was Serena's turn to tint pink. She thought Philip was . . . well, *really* nice.

"Anyway, he said Philip was going to ride with a friend he just met at camp, because he doesn't have a brother or sister, either. And then I said, well, all of my friends are riding, and then he suggested Claudette." Lucy looked down for a second. "I feel kind of ashamed that I didn't think of Claudette right away. I've been having so much fun with friends my own age that I forgot she really is a friend, too."

"Don't worry about it," Serena said. "You're good to her. Let's wash the bikes up, and by the time we're done, Roberto will be home to fix your bike. Then we'll go over to Claudette's, and you can ask her. Hopefully she'll want to ride."

"Why wouldn't she? She'll probably be thrilled!"

They arrived at Serena's house and walked the bike around back.

Serena got her tandem out of the shed and parked it next to Lucy's. "Here's a pail." She handed over a gray bucket. "Will you go inside my kitchen and squirt some soap into it from under the sink? I'll get the hose and towels out for us."

Lucy walked into Serena's house. Mrs. Romero was standing over the stove, cooking up onions and peppers. "Hello, *Lucita*." She patted Lucy's head. "I hear you're going to ride in the One Plus One this week after all."

"I sure hope so." Lucy breathed deeply. "What is that delicious smell?"

"Fajitas. Would you like to stay for lunch?"

"Yes, thank you. Serena said I could get some soap in here. We're going to wash the bikes up before Roberto comes home. He's going to fix mine for me. Then I'll be ready to ride."

Mrs. Romero handed over a curvy plastic bottle of lemon dish soap. "This should get your bike shiny. How's your mother?"

"She's fine, thanks," Lucy answered on her way out.

She let the screen door slam behind her. Venus spied her and came running. "No, Venus, don't jump!" Venus obeyed. "Good girl." She pulled out a cheese cube for Venus and the Jelly Bellies for her and Serena.

"Want one?" She opened her plastic Jelly Belly case.

"Mix me a flavor," Serena said. "I love your combinations."

Lucy picked out a new favorite. She took one Top Banana, one Chocolate Pudding, one Crushed Pineapple, one Strawberry Jam, one Very Cherry, and one Cream Soda and handed them to Serena. "Put them all in at once and chew," she instructed.

Serena popped them all into her mouth. "Yum! Banana split?"

"Yep. Delicious, eh?"

Serena nodded.

After sudsing up their bikes and then rinsing and drying them, Serena and Lucy each got on the front seat of their bikes. They stood side by side.

"It's going to be fun," Lucy said. For the first time all week, she allowed herself to believe she might really ride.

Now, if Roberto could only fix the bike.

The two of them lay on the grass with Venus for a while. Then they left her to sleep under the shade of a tree with a plastic bowl of water nearby while they went to eat lunch. Roberto joined them and afterward said, "Well, let's look at that bike!"

The three of them ran out to the back, and Roberto opened his black folding leather case with bike tools strapped inside. "I got it free when I started working at OutSpoken." His face looked older than seventeen years when he talked about his job.

Dear God, let him be able to fix it.

After a few minutes Roberto said, "I think that's it. Let's give it a ride together and see."

They wheeled Fireball out front and slipped their helmets on. Lucy rode in the front and Roberto in the back. They pedaled together, and the bike cruised along much faster than a single bike. After a couple of trips around the block, they pulled back up to the house.

"I think you're set!" Roberto said. "It's riding just fine now."

Thank you, God! And, "Thank you, Roberto."

"No problem."

Serena came out front. "I want to ride, too! I made sure Venus is safe. Should we all ride over to Claudette's house and see if she wants to take it for a spin?"

"Oh yes," Lucy said. "It would be fun for us to warm up and get used to riding together. Let's go!"

They all got on the bikes. Roberto and Serena looked so . . . well, *together* on their bike. Their shorts and shirts almost matched, even though Lucy knew they hadn't planned that. It was like they just went together.

Lucy felt a bit awkward trying to ride her big bike alone, no one at all in the back. "Come on, Fireball," she muttered as she struggled with the bike. "Let's go get Claudette."

Serena made them stop while she rearranged herself. "This seat hurts, Roberto. Can't you make it softer?"

"It's a bike seat, Serena. You don't ride that often. Don't be a baby. It's fine."

Serena frowned at him but soon cheered, and they went on their way.

This was so cool! As they rounded the corner of Marine Way, Lucy looked down the hill and saw a cruise ship anchored in the channel for the day. The water was shiny, reflecting the sun like a new quarter on a summer sidewalk.

"Are we almost there?" Serena called to Lucy. Lucy, working to keep Fireball going on her own, nodded back.

They pulled up in front of Claudette's house. Serena and Roberto waited on the sidewalk; Lucy toed the L-shaped kickstand down and walked up the small sidewalk.

She knocked on the dark wooden door. Pretty jasmine curled like doll hair around the wooden posts marking off the small porch.

Finally the door opened, but just a crack. Claudette's face peeked out. "Hi, Lucy!"

She didn't open the door any more, but Lucy could hear Claudette's puppy scurrying behind her, racing in circles, then poking his nose out, trying to escape. Also, Lucy saw a chubby brown hand push Claudette's face to the side and peek out herself. When she saw Lucy, Chantal broke out in the famous four-tooth smile.

Lucy grinned back.

"Claudette?"

Claudette came back into view. The puppy still scurried—Lucy could hear him scuffle and bark.

"I was just wondering if you'd like to ride in the One Plus One on Friday?"

Lucy couldn't see much of Claudette's face, but what she *could* see didn't look happy at all. For a full ten seconds Claudette said nothing.

A Surprise

Wednesday...

Mama mia. Is Claudette ever going to answer?

"Well?" Lucy said. "What do you think?"

A chubby hand reached around and tugged on Claudette's hair. "No!" Claudette said in a sharp voice. A little giggle came from behind the door. The dog began to bark a little more.

The hand tugged again, harder, it seemed, on Claudette's hair. "No, Chantal. The rule is no pulling hair. Why won't you obey?" She unwrapped Chantal's fingers, which had entwined themselves in Claudette's hair. The baby started to cry. The puppy barked louder.

"Well, I can't. My sister's not old enough to ride a bike yet, and we don't have a baby cart to pull behind a bike," Claudette said. "So I guess I'll just have to wait until she's older."

"But, Claudette..." Lucy began, but Duke poked his nose out the door and barked. Chantal kept crying.

"Mom!" Claudette yelled back in the house. "Help me." She turned back to Lucy. "I've got to go. Sorry about it all. I'll see you tomorrow. Maybe my mom will pay you extra now to baby-sit both of us. Bye!"

With that she shut the door in Lucy's face. From behind the thick wooden door, Lucy could still hear Chantal wailing.

Well. Lucy walked down to the curb, where Serena and Roberto looked at her expectantly.

"Is she excited that you asked her?" Serena asked.

"Not really. She says she wants to wait until her sister is older," Lucy said. "I guess most people just want to ride with their siblings. I can't blame her. I would."

Serena and Roberto stood there, quietly but kindly.

"Are you sure?" Serena said. "It's so strange. She usually wants to tag along with you on everything."

"I know," Lucy said. "But I guess that was before she had a sister." She sighed. "I think I'll go home now, if you guys don't mind."

"I can come with you," Serena offered.

"Nah. Go ahead and ride with Roberto. Will you bring Venus home in a little while, though?"

"Of course. You sure?"

"I'm sure."

Roberto and Serena took off down the street, pedaling. Lucy got back on Fireball. Instead of riding toward home, though, she headed toward her dad's office.

Shoulda thought about Claudette having her own sister now. I can't really blame her, after all. I mean, I haven't given her much attention this summer, really. And I'd probably be different if I had my own sister, too.

But I'd still invite Claudette somehow. I would.

Halfway there, Lucy noticed the bike pitching forward a little bit. Then she heard a *flap-flap* sound. Lucy sighed. *Flat tire. Must have been a slow leak.*

She got off and walked, but the tire still *flap-flap*ped through the center of town. She came to Sweet Dreams, the ice-cream shop Jake's family owned. She parked the tandem out front.

"Ice cream?" Jake's sister asked Lucy politely as she stood near the counter. Lucy looked all around but didn't see Jake. She was kind of half hoping he'd have another great idea, or maybe at least a friendly smile.

"Just a Dr Pepper, please." Lucy pulled a dollar bill out of her pocket and took the pop outside with her. She sat at one of the little heart-shaped tables with two chairs. The familiar cola fizz bubbled across her tongue and down her throat.

Lucy's friend Erica rode by with her mother in a golf cart. When they stopped at the stop sign, Erica called out, "Hey, Luce! Is that yours?" Erica pointed to Fireball.

Lucy nodded.

"All right! I'm so glad! See you Friday!" Erica's mom *onk-onk*ed the horn and took off. The horn sounded like a goose with a cold. Lucy waved; there was no time to explain what was really going on.

Lucy finished her Dr Pepper, took one more hopeful look for Jake, and tossed her bottle into the recycle bin.

She kicked up the kickstand and thought about stopping by OutSpoken to buy a new tube for the wheel. But why? She may just as well park the bike in the back room of her dad's office, where it would wait till next year.

Lucy looked down the street. People walked together. Flowers grew together. Birds flew together. She held tightly on to Fireball and made it to her dad's office.

Thank you, God, that at least Julie didn't walk by right now. Julie lived right up the street from the office.

She opened the office door. She could see Mr. Kingsley on the phone in his office. He looked up and waved to her; she waved back. He already had a picture of Chantal added to the one of Claudette in his office.

Lucy's dad was on the phone, too, but he signaled to her to wait. In a minute he came out. "What'cha doing? Did Roberto fix the bike?"

"Yes."

"So why is it here?"

Lucy put her finger to her lips. She didn't want Mr. Kingsley to overhear them. "Let's go out back."

They went on the patio of the office, which used to be a house. It looked over the channel. Lucy could see little boats sailing in and out. It had been a while since they'd boated.

"Well?" her dad asked. He looked at his watch.

"I asked Claudette if she wanted to ride with me. She said she can't and practically shut the door in my face. She did, really, shut the door in my face. Even though I know the dog was trying to escape."

"Are you sure she doesn't want to ride?"

"Yes." Lucy opened her Jelly Belly case. "And now Fireball has a flat tire."

"Who is Fireball?"

Lucy smiled. "The tandem."

"Ah." Dad scratched his beard. "I'll still ride with you. Or Mom will. If you want."

"I know," Lucy said. "I've got to think about it, okay? I just hadn't counted on this happening." She popped a Sizzling Cinnamon into her mouth, in honor of Fireball, and snapped the case shut.

"Okay." Dad pulled her into a hug and then stepped back. "I have to get back to work, but you go home, rest, and read for a bit. Train Venus. I've got a surprise for you tonight—something I think you'll really like."

"A surprise?"

"A surprise," he promised. "Now I'd best get back to work."

"Okay," Lucy said. She radioed her mother that she was on her way home and began walking.

What could the surprise be?

Hey . . . maybe Dad has been talking with Mr. Kingsley about adoption!

Hope

Wednesday afternoon and evening . . .

When Lucy walked into the house, her mom was still at work, classical music humming through the walls and closed door. Lucy knocked on the living room door and then went in.

"I'm home," she said.

Mom set her brush down. "Did you just get home? Have you been to your room yet?"

"Yes and no," Lucy said. "I'm heading up there now." She turned to walk away, then stopped and turned back around. "I asked Claudette today if she wanted to ride in the One Plus One with me. She said no."

Mom reached out and tucked a section of hair behind Lucy's ear. "I'm sorry, honey. After last night I thought you'd planned to ride with Dad. Did she say why?"

"I think she just wants to wait for her sister. I can't blame her. I wish I had a sister. It's just . . . well, I guess I didn't realize how much I wanted to go with Claudette after all. It'd be like old times, every summer. I thought I hated that. I guess I didn't."

"I'm sorry." Mom stood there for a second. "Hey! How about I ride with you—just the two of us, mother and daughter—since we aren't going to L.A. together?"

It was a big deal to say that, Lucy knew. It might mean Mom wouldn't get her painting done in time. And she wasn't even worried about the new client. She was worried about Lucy. But Dad might be counting on riding with Lucy, too. He'd said he wanted to. She didn't want to hurt the feelings of one by saying yes to the other. She'd better think for a bit on how to handle it. And did she even want to ride with a parent when everyone else was going with another kid? But if she didn't, would she rather sit out and miss out on the fun? Maybe Roberto would have to work at the bike shop at the last minute, she thought wistfully.

Hmm. All Lucy said for now was, "If it's okay with you, I told Dad I'll think about it till tomorrow. I want to take a little more time, okay?"

"Sure," Mom said. "I'm so glad to see you thinking through things." She gave Lucy a peck on the cheek. "I understand. Come and get me when Dad has the food on the table, and I'll take a break with you for dinner."

"Okay."

Lucy played with Venus for a few minutes, and then Venus followed her upstairs.

When she walked into her room, Lucy saw that her mom had made her bed and dusted off her dresser. A pair of daisies clipped from the backyard sprang from an old jelly jar. Lucy smiled. *Even though Mom had only a few minutes, she spent them on me.* The lone wilted balloon, left over from Chantal's welcome home, sat still and smooshy like an old orange next to the African violet on Lucy's dresser.

Taped onto her mirror was a new pencil sketch of Lucy, her mom and dad, and Venus.

Lucy sat down and read for a while till her dad hollered up the stairs. "Lucy!"

Oh yeah! The surprise!

Lucy ran down the stairs and met her dad in the kitchen. Something smelled good and garlicky. *Garlic toast?*

She knocked on the living room door. "Come on, Mom. Dinner!"

Mom followed her into the kitchen. When they sat down, her dad presented a platter with some brown shells on it and long, thin forks.

"Oh. Um, Dad? What are these?"

"Snails! In garlic butter, of course," he said. "I know you like to try new things, and you'd been thinking that pizza and cheese sandwiches were boring. I remembered that you'd liked the oysters, and I thought, why not?" He grinned. "My surprise for my culinary adventuress!"

Very careful to keep the smile on her face and make no comment about the university professor language, Lucy said, "Thanks."

Well, the surprise was *not* that he had talked about adoption with Mr. Kingsley. But when Lucy looked at her parents' earnest faces, she knew how hard they tried.

Lucy dug a snail out of the shell with the long silver

fork, its two tines sticking into the firm flesh. She pulled the snail meat out and stared at it before committing it to her mouth. It kind of looked like shrimp. Finally she popped it in. It kind of tasted like garlic shrimp, too. She chewed and swallowed. It wasn't too bad.

"It's pretty good," she said.

Dad poked one and ate it. "I like them, too."

Mom smiled and took a bite out of one corner. After chewing that much, she ate the rest of the snail. "It won't replace spaghetti and meatballs, but anything with garlic butter is okay with me."

The three of them ate. Lucy noticed her Mom looking at her watch once.

"Thanks for the pencil sketch, Mom, and for straightening my room."

Mom brightened. "Remember when you were a little girl, and when you'd help me, I'd draw a five-minute sketch for you?"

"Yeah. I kept them in my diary."

"I wanted to do one for you on a break today, to celebrate Venus being in the picture. And because you're growing into such a good helper."

Lucy wondered if her mom could add a new baby, too, if the time came.

"Thanks," was all she said.

"I'm sorry about Claudette not riding with you," Dad said in between bites.

"Me too," Lucy said. She speared another snail.

No one said anything for a minute, and even though Lucy had not meant to bring it up yet, a few words snuck out before she could stop them. "So why don't I have a brother or sister?"

Mom looked at Dad, not her watch, this time. "Well, it's not very complicated," she said. "I do know how you feel, Luce, I really do. I'm an only child, too, remember?"

Lucy tried to keep her voice even. "Then I'm surprised that you would have wanted me to be that way."

"We didn't want you to be that way at first," Dad jumped in. "We tried to have you for quite a few years and were so happy when we finally had you in our lives."

"And afterward," Mom continued, "we kept trying a long time. But we never had any more kids. Nothing happened. Just because a couple wants a baby doesn't mean it always happens. So we went on with our lives and enjoyed you and felt blessed and stopped dwelling on it."

"Oh."

"Does it make you sad?" Mom asked. "Still?"

"Sometimes." Lucy chewed some more snail meat, determined not to say anything more. If she did, adoption might come up, and she didn't want to spill the idea before she had the packet—her ammo—in hand. The adoption packet, with all the answers and pictures of cute babies, was sure to convince them. Hadn't her mother asked Chantal if there were any other cuties like her where she'd come from? She wouldn't be able to resist. And, of course, the nice dinner would be prepared. Mom and Dad's stressful week would be behind them.

And Lucy had noticed that her mom had never said she didn't want another baby, only that one hadn't come.

"This was great, Dad," Lucy said. "Did Mom tell you

I wanted to plan a special dinner for you two on Friday night, just the three of us? You'll be done with the water bottle booth for One Plus One, and Mom's painting will be done."

"Sounds good, Sparky." Dad folded his napkin.

"Will you take me to the store tonight so I can get the stuff?"

He nodded. "Okay."

"You can wait in the golf cart while I shop. That way my stuff will be a surprise, but you'll be right outside waiting, okay?"

Dad nodded.

Mom cleared the table; then she went back to work.

Lucy ran back upstairs to get her sweat jacket.

She looked at her mood ring. Warm and blue.

"I'm ready, Dad." Lucy and her dad climbed into the golf cart and rode to the store.

"How about if I give you my debit card?"

"Wow! Yeah!" Dad had *never* let her use his debit card on her own before.

"Dinner stuff only, okay?"

"Promise."

Lucy stepped out of the cart and into the store. Up and down the aisles she wandered. What to make?

Hey! Mom loves spaghetti and meatballs. And that was something Lucy could make. She grabbed a green box of noodles and a couple of jars of pasta sauce. In the frozen foods department she grabbed a box of meatballs.

On the inside of the freezer door she wrote *Girl Power!* backward in the frost and circled it with a heart before she closed the door. She giggled as she walked away.

Oh yeah. Garlic bread. She headed back to the freezer department. Someone was adding more exclamation points to her comments. She smiled.

Now a brownie mix for dessert. And lemonade. It would all be perfect.

She stepped up to the cashier and ran Dad's debit card through the slot. After paying, she headed back to the golf cart. Dad clicked off his recorder.

"Ready?"

"Ready." Lucy looked down at the brown bags, pleased that she'd asked for paper so he couldn't see through them.

They puttered the couple of blocks home, and Lucy put the stuff away. Then she went to sit on the porch swing for a few minutes and looked at the summer sky.

The stars were scattered across the denim sky like rhinestones. She looked beyond them and thought of the Lord. Then she thought over Claudette's response today and let a tear slide down her cheek. She brushed it away.

"I'm not sure I even want to baby-sit silly Claudette and that silly baby tomorrow," she said out loud.

She sat rocking in the swing, looking at the lawn. It wasn't thick grass—a little scraggly. But wild yellow flowers were buttoned into it, and it brought a smile to her face. Something simple.

"I don't really think Claudette is silly, Lord. Not Chantal, either. I'm sorry for saying it. It's just that I didn't expect Claudette to say no. She really does feel a lot more like a friend this year than I had expected. And now I'll feel weird showing up with one of my parents when everyone else is going with a kid."

She drew her knees up toward her. Another midsummer night. Just like the duet for four hands she and Mariette had played Tuesday night.

Tonight, Lucy still felt four hands dealing with this situation. Hers and God's.

She felt peaceful and full and closer to Him than she had for a while, just knowing His hands were there, too.

A tandem bike rode by, two sisters on it. The day after tomorrow the rally would be here. And Mrs. Chin would arrive with the packet.

A Decision

"You've promised to be at Claudette's house in fifteen minutes." Mom poked her head into Lucy's room. Lucy was just finishing making her bed and giving her violet a drink of water. Amazingly, the plant hadn't yet died! Lucy was famous for her black thumb. In the past, all of her plants had died quick deaths.

"I know, I'm on my way." Lucy grabbed her purse on the way downstairs. She stopped and rubbed Venus for a while. "I'll be back in a couple of hours, girl. I can't handle a girl and a baby and their dog, plus you." The whole thing seemed a bit overwhelming now. "I hope you understand." Venus licked Lucy's hand, and Lucy smiled back. Then she headed out the door.

The day was already hot, and the warm, salty air smelled like fresh popcorn. Tomorrow was the One Plus One—today was the last day to decide if she'd ride or not. She'd have to make the call by this afternoon.

She arrived at Claudette's and rang the bell. This time Mrs. Kingsley opened the door. "Hi, Lucy!"

"Hello, Mrs. Kingsley." Lucy stepped inside. *No chaos today. Whew.*

"I'm going to be downtown shopping for a little bit and mailing off some papers. I should be back in about two hours. Okay?"

Lucy nodded and headed toward the bedroom, where Claudette was patiently teaching Chantal some English words. She'd point to a doll and say, "Doll." Claudette never raised her voice or got tired before Chantal got the word. Lucy smiled. Claudette had a marshmallow heart after all.

Claudette looked up as Lucy walked into the room. "Oh, yay, someone here to play with *me* for a change!" she said. "If we can find any space in here with all these little kid toys." She giggled.

"I'll help you," Lucy said. She sat on the floor with the two of them.

"Did you ever notice that people have an M for a nose?" Claudette asked.

"What?!"

"Well, look." Claudette pointed at Chantal's nose. "If you start at the bottom and go around one nostril and then the other, it looks like a letter M. Kind of like McDonald's. Want to see mine?" She tipped her head back.

Lucy laughed. "No, Claudette, I don't want to look up your nose. Thanks anyway, you goofy!"

Claudette laughed with her.

"What do you want to play?"

"Will you do my hair?" Claudette asked. "Nobody has had any time to do my hair since the baby came. It's too hard, my mom says. It's all she can do to keep up. So that means my hair doesn't get done and my games don't get played."

Lucy nodded and set Chantal next to the bed with some blocks to play with. Lucy got Claudette's hair stuff out of the drawer and did a few pin curls.

Chantal reached over and grabbed the box of bobby pins, spilling them on the floor. Then she grabbed a handful of them and tried to stick them into her mouth.

"No!" Lucy said. She pried open Chantal's hand and took the bobby pins away. "You could choke!"

Chantal began to cry. Claudette scooped up the rest of the bobby pins and sat on her bed. "Putting it up here is the only way to keep her out of my stuff."

Lucy tried to get Chantal to quiet down. Blocks didn't work. Dolls didn't work. Finally she handed her a box of Kleenex and let her pull out one after another. It was the only thing that kept her quiet. Lucy would probably have to pay Mrs. Kingsley back for the Kleenex.

While Chantal scattered Kleenex, Lucy finished twirling Claudette's hair up in bobby pins, and then she sprayed them wet.

"Let's let them dry for a bit. When we take out the pins, your hair will be curly. I'll spray them so they don't fall out right away. And then we can go for a walk around the block with the baby in her stroller. Okay?"

Claudette nodded. "But remember, she has to have a drink of water every two hours or she'll get dehydrated."

Lucy smiled. "All right, you big sister, you."

Claudette smiled back. "All right with *me*, big sister. Because you kind of are to me, you know."

Lucy patted Claudette's pinned-up head and grinned in spite of herself. "If you say so. Want to give Duke a bath and then take Chantal for a walk?"

"Yes!" Claudette clapped her hands, so Chantal clapped her hands, too, sippy cup and all. The three of them headed outside. Lucy made sure the gate was tightly closed, then got out a bucket, some towels, and some shampoo.

She ran some warm water from the kitchen tap, and then they trapped Claudette's puppy in a corner. Claudette held on to him while Lucy sudsed him up. Before she could get the dog rinsed, though, Chantal knocked over the bucket of water.

Lucy sighed. It was an accident, after all. But she'd have to go back into the house for more water. So she carried Chantal on one hip and the bucket in the other arm. She opened the screen door with her elbow while Claudette held on to the soapy puppy, who was making very unhappy barking noises.

Lucy returned with more water, and after a few minutes they got the dog rinsed off. The puppy ran away and shook for all he was worth. It was okay, though, the dog was clean and rinsed by then. Chantal broke out laughing again, taking her sippy cup out of her mouth. Lucy looked at her watch. She was exhausted. And she'd only been there for one hour.

Lucy looked at the dog. He would love a walk, she knew. But with the baby . . . Lucy just couldn't do it all.

"Let's leave Duke here while we go for our walk around the block. I don't want to have to watch him, too, and he'll get a good drying off."

"Okay," Claudette agreed.

Lucy sat on the grass next to Claudette and, one by one, pulled the bobby pins out of Claudette's hair. The shiny curls had dried in the sun, and now they spilled like a tangle over Claudette's head.

"How does it look?"

"Pretty," Lucy said. For the first time this summer she noticed that Claudette was growing up, too. "And kind of grown-up."

"Does it make me look like you? With the curls and all?"

Lucy looked it over. Claudette's hair was still a bit longer, since Lucy had had hers cut. But not too much. And while it wasn't the same strawberry blond, it was a brownish red.

"Kind of. Yes, it kind of does." For some reason that made Claudette's not wanting to ride in the One Plus One even more painful.

Claudette ran her fingers through her curls. Chantal reached her arms up toward Lucy and tried out her new word. "Doll."

Lucy picked her up. "Yes, you are a doll. Let's go for a walk, little doll, okay?" The three of them went into the house. Lucy felt bad leaving the dog in the back. The puppy whined when they left, but there was no other solution.

She took the stroller out to the sidewalk, and they

headed out to enjoy the day. Lucy made sure Chantal's bonnet was tied over her head so she wouldn't get too much sun.

As they walked down the street, several tandems rode by. *Getting ready for tomorrow,* Lucy supposed. She sighed.

To her surprise Claudette sighed, too. "I wish I could go on that tandem bike ride tomorrow. It looks like so much fun."

Lucy stopped the stroller dead in its tracks. "WHAT? Are you kidding? I asked you yesterday if you wanted to go on this with me, and you said no. That you wanted to wait for Chantal! I was waiting outside with the bike and everything."

Now Claudette stopped in her tracks. "Lucy, you did *not* ask me if I wanted to go *with you.* You just asked me if I wanted to go. And I thought I couldn't, because on Saturday *you* said that it was only a ride for brothers and sisters. And my sister isn't old enough yet. I wasn't going to break the rules, you know."

Lucy thought about Claudette's watch beeping every four hours for feeding the baby. And her not squeezing the baby too tight and wanting to make sure Chantal had water every two hours. No, Claudette was not one to want to break the rules. If she had thought that was what the rule was.

"So you do want to go? Because friends can ride together. I asked because . . . well, because I don't have a sister."

They kept walking, but Claudette turned to walk facing

Lucy. "You said people could ride with friends. Are we friends, really?"

"Yes." Lucy looked at Claudette, puzzled.

"I have a sister now. But sometimes I feel lonely because I don't have a best friend."

Lucy saw Claudette's Wired for Christ necklace sparkling in the sunlight—the necklace Lucy had given Claudette some weeks ago. A friendship necklace.

"Well, I'll be your best friend all day tomorrow for the race, okay?" Lucy said.

"The whole day?!"

"The whole day," Lucy promised. Just then she remembered—Fireball had a flat tire. Was there enough time to get it fixed?

"Let's get home and call Roberto to see if he can fix the flat tire on the tandem." Lucy spun the stroller around, and they headed back toward Claudette's house.

"And plan what we're going to wear, right? Can we be matchies?"

Lucy smiled. "Kind of matchies—nothing totally weird, okay?"

"Okay," Claudette happily agreed.

Once they got back to the Kingsleys, Lucy called her mom.

"Mom? Claudette wants to ride after all. Is that okay with you? I mean, maybe you were really looking forward to it. I don't want to hurt your feelings."

"Oh no," her mother said. "I'm very happy for you, honey. I'll work at the booth as we had planned. And you get to go with a friend!"

"I'm really happy, too," Lucy answered. "For both me *and* Claudette." Lucy asked if it would be okay if they went to their dads' office when Claudette's mom returned, to check Fireball over and somehow get the flat fixed.

"Sure, sure, see you later. Keep your radio on, please." Then her mom hung up.

Claudette spent the next hour planning their outfits—putting together colors that they both had and that Lucy would agree to wear. Chantal, thankfully, took a nap.

"It's the only time of day we rest," Claudette confided. "I don't want to say it when she's awake in case she understands and it would hurt her feelings, but sometimes the quiet is nice."

They finally settled on blue jean shorts, the blue T-shirts, if they could get them, and white sneakers.

"But I'm not wearing two different-colored socks, Claudette. I draw the line at that."

Claudette, who *always* wore two different-colored socks, agreed for this one day to wear a matching pair.

Mrs. Kingsley came home and took over Chantal. Lucy explained about the Kleenex and was relieved when Mrs. Kingsley laughed it off. Happy now, Lucy and Claudette raced together to their dads' office. Would there still be enough time to register for the race? Would there be T-shirts left?

They ran in, but both of their dads were busy. After waiting a few minutes, they explained their plan.

Next Lucy called Roberto. "He said to bring Fireball down and he'd see if there was a tube for the tire," she told her dad after hanging up. "He hoped so but couldn't promise. With the big race this week, they are running very low on supplies."

Mr. Kingsley said he would run downtown and register the girls and get them T-shirts if any were left.

Lucy's dad wheeled Fireball out and set it on the sidewalk. Lucy hopped on the front seat—in the captain's position. Claudette hopped on the backseat—in the stoker's position.

Well, she tried to, at least.

As Lucy looked back in horror, she saw that Claudette was too short for the bike. She couldn't reach the handlebars and the pedals at the same time. If she leaned forward for the handlebars, her feet wouldn't reach the pedals. And if she reached the pedals, she couldn't lean far enough forward to hold on.

"Here! Try the front seat." Lucy hopped off and wiped the sweat off of her forehead with the sleeve of her shirt.

Claudette gave it a try, but the captain's position was even worse.

Claudette jumped off the bike and buried her face in her hands. "OH NO!"

Lucy felt like crying, too. "Oh no!"

Adversity

Thursday afternoon . . .

"Well . . ." Lucy's dad started to speak.

"What? Do you have an idea?" Lucy asked.

Claudette pulled her hands away from her face.

"Well, not really."

Lucy's hopes felt like Fireball's deflated tire.

"But let's not panic. How can we solve this problem? It's just a problem to be solved, nothing more." Dad closed his eyes.

"Well," Lucy said. "Why not ask Roberto? Maybe there's something at OutSpoken that can help us."

Dad nodded. "Surely Claudette isn't the only younger girl riding."

"Right, that's true!" Lucy began to feel jazzed again. "Because Betsy is riding with her sister, Michelle, who is the same age as Claudette."

"Maybe they have a different kind of bike?" Claudette suggested.

"Maybe," Lucy said. "But maybe not. Let's wait till your dad gets back and see if he was able to register us. If not, there's no sense going down to OutSpoken anyway. If so, we'll race over to see if Roberto or someone he works with can help us."

"I pray that he can," Claudette said. She reached out for Lucy's hand. Lucy squeezed it.

"I hope so, too, Claudette."

The two of them played a computer game for a while, waiting for Mr. Kingsley to come back. Claudette wanted to play a dress-up doll disk. Then Claudette watched while Lucy wrote some music online with the online program.

While Claudette was playing doll dress-up, Lucy looked at the sign above the computer. It said *Overcoming Adversity Always Builds a Team.* She smiled.

She and Claudette hoped to be a team, anyway.

After half an hour of fiddling with the computer, Lucy was hungry. "Wish I had some Jelly Bellies," she said.

"Here." Claudette drew a tin from her pocket. "Want a mint? I've already had three today, and the container says not to eat more than four in a day. Too much spearmint oil. But you can have some."

She opened the tin and neatly folded the paper back. Lucy reached in and took one. *Not bad. Not really satisfying, though.*

Finally Mr. Kingsley walked in. "Here you are!" He waved two T-shirts back and forth in the air like distress flags. Claudette ran up to him.

"Dad, I can't fit on the bike. We need to go down to OutSpoken and see if Roberto can fix it."

Lucy's stomach rumbled loudly, and they all laughed. Her dad handed her some money. "Why don't you get some lunch at Sweet Dreams while you're at it?"

"Thanks."

The two girls walked Fireball down to the bike shop. "Do you think they'll be able to fix it? I mean, do they have a booster seat or something? No, that wouldn't work. It will just make me farther away from the pedals."

"Roberto's pretty good. Let's see what he finds out."

They walked the bike into a *very* busy shop. Serena was there, too, and she hugged Lucy and Claudette.

"Guess what?" Lucy said. "Claudette and I are all signed up to ride in the One Plus One together."

"Hooray!" Serena said.

"But," Claudette said, "there are a couple of problems."

"Uh-oh."

Roberto came over then. "I can take care of the flat tire easily."

Whew!

"But about the other problem." Lucy looked at Serena. "Claudette can't reach both the handlebars and the pedals the way the bike is. She has to lean too far forward, and then her feet don't reach."

Roberto had Claudette get on the back of Fireball. He measured her both toward the handlebars and also meeting the pedals.

"Well, there are a couple of things. We can get her a kiddie crank."

"What's that?" Claudette said. "Does it hurt?"

"No." Roberto laughed. "It's a special attachment that

allows the pedals to be several inches closer to the seat. Or else we can get you a different stoker stem, one that brings the handlebars closer to you. I think that would be best. But . . ."

"Are they expensive?" Lucy asked.

"Not too much. But here's the real problem."

Lucy sat down. Claudette and Serena joined her.

"I don't have any more of either of them. With the One Plus One happening tomorrow, there have been a lot of people wanting parts."

Oh no. She'd gotten so close to riding in the rally with a friend.

Then, in her head, she heard her dad's voice from earlier. *Let's not panic.* "How can we solve this problem? It's just a problem to be solved, nothing more," she said aloud.

"I can call over town and see if any of the shops we work with have parts. It'll take me some time, because I'm busy. Why don't you come back in half an hour and I'll let you know."

"Okay." Lucy radioed her mom to make sure it was okay to have Roberto order the parts if they found them. She said she'd be eating at Sweet Dreams with Serena and Claudette and would be home soon.

The three of them walked over to Sweet Dreams. Serena and Claudette sat at the table. Lucy could tell by looking at Claudette's face that she was happy to be a part of the older girls eating lunch. "I'll go order for us," Lucy said.

Jake was behind the counter.

"Hey, if it isn't the famous Dr Pepper!" He smiled, and

the smile was real. "Here. My dad got some new Jelly Bellies in last night. Tell me what you think."

He handed Lucy a paper cup filled with beans. Lucy popped one into her mouth. *Yum.* "Juicy Pear."

"My favorite," Jake said.

And my new second favorite, Lucy thought.

She ordered cheeseburgers and fries and pop for all of them.

"I see that girl is sitting out there with you and Serena," Jake said.

"Yeah. I invited her to ride, like you suggested. Thanks."

"No problem."

"Now we just have to see if some parts can come in from over town in order to have her reach the pedals. Roberto is calling now."

"I hope it all works out okay," Jake said. "It would be fun to have you riding with all of us."

Lucy smiled. "I think so, too."

She rejoined her friends on the patio, and after scarfing down their lunches, they walked back to OutSpoken.

"Maybe," Roberto said when he saw them.

"Maybe?"

"I found someone who thinks he can put his hand on a part. If he can get it this afternoon, he'll put it on a late ferry tonight or an early one tomorrow. You'll have to stop by in the morning and just see if it's arrived. I'm sorry. It's a really crazy time for us, and I can't promise anything. I'll call if I think about it. Or if I'm not swamped."

"Okay," Lucy said.

"And," Serena told her brother, "I have a package coming in tomorrow on the ferry, too. Don't open it. It's for *my eyes only* before the rally."

"What is it?" Lucy asked.

"A surprise." Serena giggled. "You'll have to wait till tomorrow to see."

Walking home, Lucy could barely keep in her skin about tomorrow. Would the part be there? Would she and Claudette get to ride together after all? After all this she wouldn't want to ride without Claudette—it would be too hurtful to her. And then there was Mrs. Chin. She'd be by with the packet in the afternoon.

Lucy had better make the brownies tonight for tomorrow night's dinner. Just in case.

A Surprising Arrival

Friday . . . D Day!

Lucy got up and put on her blue T-shirt and jean shorts. Had Roberto gotten the parts in time? She could only hope. After brushing her teeth and teasing some curls out of her hair, she went downstairs to get Venus out of bed.

"Hey—no crying this morning?" Lucy smiled as Venus just licked her hand and came right out. Venus really felt at home now. The two of them went out back and played catch for a while so Venus would get some exercise before they were gone all day.

"Eggs?" Lucy came into the kitchen.

"I want you to have a healthy breakfast before you ride," Mom said. "And since I don't have to cook dinner tonight, I thought I'd do this."

Lucy dug into her breakfast, not wanting to remind her mom about the One Plus One pancake breakfast after she'd tried so hard.

Dinner was *all* planned. The brownies were already baked. Now all she needed was the secret packet from Mrs. Chin.

Dad had already gone ahead to make sure the university's water bottle booth was well stocked and that the water would be iced before the swarm of riders buzzed in. Claudette's dad was going to meet him there. "We'll go down to OutSpoken first, and then after the race begins, Mrs. Kingsley, Chantal, and I will go to the booth," Lucy's mom said. "Then I've got to get back here, put a few finishing touches on my painting, and— voilá! I'm done."

The girls would have to stay at the booth, too, if Roberto didn't receive a kiddie crank or a new stoker stem.

Lucy polished off her eggs and slipped a couple of scrambles to Venus on her way out. They locked the door behind them.

Two bluebirds, like the ones in Cinderella, whistled to them on their way, a cheerful song that set the tone for the morning.

"Do you think Roberto got the bike parts, Mom?"

"I hope so," her mother said. "I'll still ride with you if he didn't."

Lucy shook her head. "I don't want to leave Claudette out."

When they arrived at OutSpoken, Serena, Claudette, Chantal, and Mrs. Kingsley were waiting. Chantal had a light blue jumper on and was crying. Her mother looked distressed as she tried to calm the baby down. Claudette just looked embarrassed.

"I wanted her to match us," Claudette said as Lucy arrived, drawing attention to the baby's clothes and not her tantrum.

Lucy smiled. She'd probably want her sister to match, too—although she could do without the crying attack!

Down the street people were gathering for the pancake breakfast. "Oh! I'd forgotten the pancakes," Lucy's mom said. "I'm sorry."

"It's okay." Lucy patted her stomach. "I can always fit one pancake in there." She scanned the crowd. *Erica and Amy! Jenny!* She waved. The smell of fresh batter meeting a greasy griddle coated the air.

When they opened the door to the store, Roberto was there working hard. When he saw Lucy, he gave her a thumbs-up.

"Hooray!" Claudette said. "He got the part!"

Joy surged all through Lucy like a full-blast hose let loose on a summer lawn. It was going to happen. It was really going to happen after all!

Roberto attached the new stoker stem to the handlebars; they seemed to be the biggest problem. After he got them tightened, Claudette got on.

"I can reach. I can reach!"

"Don't go too fast at first," Roberto warned. "It takes a bit of time to get used to the bike."

"Don't worry," Lucy replied. "Too many hills to get going *too* fast. We'll take it nice and slow at first. We're not used to tandems."

Lucy and Claudette rented a Tandem-Talk—earphones and mouthpieces that each of them could wear so they could hear each other as they rode.

Roberto came over and handed a brown box to Serena. "Okay, this arrived for you," he said. "Are you ready to share the surprise?"

Serena giggled and opened the box. From it she withdrew . . . a sheepskin bike seat. "Very padded," she noted and giggled again.

"You and your bike seat," he said. "You'll be the only one out there with a padded bike seat. I'm going to look like I'm riding a sissy bike!" The girls giggled, and Roberto rolled his eyes.

"Let's go," Lucy said. "Now we've *all* got everything we need."

The four of them left the shop and headed toward the pancake breakfast on their bikes. The moms went up to the water bottle booth after Roberto promised he'd keep an eye on all three girls.

Serena and Lucy talked for a minute; Claudette was silent. As they rode a bit farther, Claudette whispered into the Tandem-Talk, "Don't forget you said you'd be my best friend all day today!" It buzzed in Lucy's ear.

Lucy whispered back, "Don't worry, I won't forget."

They got closer to the pancakes and pulled the bikes to a stop. Claudette got off and said, "This is the best day ever. You're going to be my best friend, and after the race Mrs. Chin is coming for lunch."

Lucy nearly knocked Fireball over as she turned to

Claudette. "FOR LUNCH? I thought she was coming for dinner. Later this afternoon."

Claudette looked at her. "Who told you that? Do you know Mrs. Chin?"

Lucy said nothing for a minute. "Are you sure, Claudette?"

"I'm sure. She called last night."

Lucy took a deep breath and headed toward the blueberry pancakes. Maybe Mrs. Chin would just leave the package on the steps.

☂ ☂ ☂

After the breakfast each team got a cue card that told what the race path was like, where the hills were, and where the stops would be. Claudette and Lucy looked it over as their friends buddied around and looked at their cue cards, too.

"Look at that!" Serena pointed to a tandem bike that was side-by-side instead of one in front of the other. "Aren't those cool? Roberto sold some at OutSpoken this year. They're called sociables."

"Cool," Lucy said. "And those ones, with trailers." She pointed to a big brother and sister on a tandem pulling a little cart behind them. In the cart was a preschool girl wearing her own little helmet.

Erica and Amy rode up with their sisters. Betsy and Michelle came to join them, each of them wearing bright pink bike helmets. Even Julie and her brother, Jeffrey, rode alongside.

"Hi," Julie said to Lucy.

"Hi," Lucy said back. She noticed that their bike was a bit old, but even they had matching helmets, kind of.

"I'm glad you're riding today," Julie said.

Lucy smiled warmly. "Thanks for encouraging me to come—on the beach last week. It meant a lot."

Julie smiled a quick smile and turned to talk with other friends.

The organizer fired the starting shot into the air, and the bikers took off. Lucy and Claudette got on their bike. It wobbled a bit at first, but they soon learned the rhythm of staying together. After they figured it out, they were able to stay in the pack with their other friends. They pedaled together, keeping a beat, it seemed to Lucy.

A duet. She smiled.

As they rode, they chattered away about the road, the bike, the scenery, and everything around them through their Tandem-Talk. The scenery blended together to the side like one of Lucy's mom's watercolors. It was a new perspective from a typical slow walk or a speedy golf cart.

Soon they reached a big hill that would lead to the first stop. The eucalyptus trees lining the road smelled like chest rub; it made the air seem cold and minty.

"Keep pedaling," Lucy encouraged Claudette. She ground her knees around and around, too, trying to make it up the hill without walking. When they got to the top, they stopped for a view of the channel, lovely as a painting and fresh as the day. Each person who stopped got a sticker for her helmet. Lucy stuck one on Claudette's for her, and Claudette did the same for Lucy.

"Ready?" Serena called to them.

"Ready, Miss Sheepskin," Lucy teased. They caught up and rode beside each other. That way Lucy and Serena could chat some, too. Claudette piped up through the headphones or chatted with Roberto.

The second stop was right in front of the town's horse ranch. "Not like Carla's, eh?" Serena said.

Lucy smiled. "Well, kind of, now that Carla's ranch looks so cool." The two of them, with Julie, had tidied it up last week.

"We might be in a commercial," Lucy told Claudette. "Next week."

Claudette wailed, "Oh, I go away for two weeks and all the good stuff happens. Plus, I'll probably have to stay home and play with Chantal. Maybe I can come and watch one day."

Lucy nodded. "Maybe. Ready to go, kiddo?"

They attached horsetails, which Rancher Bill had handed out to everyone, to the rear of Claudette's seat.

"Next stop is ours," Lucy said through Claudette's headphones. "The university water bottles!"

They pedaled through a street of antique houses; several older ladies stood outside and clapped as they all rode by. Lucy looked over at Serena, who grinned, and then to the other side. Betsy and Michelle rode up on that side, and Claudette began chatting with Michelle. The two of them giggled and joked.

A friend for Claudette.

They came to the little set-aside in the trees that the university used to set up a safe place to get the water bottles. "The spring of learning," Lucy's dad had joked.

Dad needed some new jokes.

As they came close, Claudette buzzed through the headphones, "Hey, Lucy, look! There's the water booth!"

Lucy gaped as they rode up. Her parents were there behind the booth with Claudette's parents. And a woman holding Chantal.

Mrs. Chin?

Lucy and Claudette were among the last to the booth because they were among the last riders. Lucy didn't know if she could even get close to her mom and dad. Maybe that was better.

"Is that Mrs. Chin from the adoption agency?" she asked Claudette. The lady was holding a smiling Chantal. They were standing next to Lucy's mother.

"Yep!" Claudette said.

Uh-oh.

SOS

Friday . . .

Lucy looked at her mom. Her mother caught her eye but just smiled, her hands already full with water bottles. On a warm morning, and after a lot of hills, the water was a popular item. Lucy waved back.

Mama mia.

"Claudette, why don't you just go up and get us some water?" Lucy suggested. "I'll stay with the bike."

"Okay." Claudette moved forward through the crowd, got some water bottles, and walked back to the bike.

"I couldn't even say hi," she said. "Too many people. Mrs. Chin is holding Chantal. She's happy, at least. My mom was worried she'd be crying when Mrs. Chin came to check on us."

"Did you hear them talking about anything in particular?"

"No." Claudette handed over Lucy's water bottle.

"Good."

"Why are you so red? Are you hot?"

"Yes," Lucy said. "I'm hot." *So far, so good.* Now she just needed to finish the race and then get with Mrs. Chin. Alone. As long as nothing came out first.

Okay, Lucy, she talked herself down. *Pay attention to the race. You can deal with Mrs. Chin later. Finish up here first. You've waited for a long time for this.*

They tossed their empty bottles into one of the recycling bins placed all along the route, and then everyone headed down the homestretch. Lucy and Claudette hopped onto Fireball and headed down the road, too.

Riding time was thinking time. Did Mrs. Chin bring the package? Would Lucy's parents think that a baby sister for Lucy was a good idea, too? Did they want another child as much as Lucy did?

They drew near the finish line—just a few more minutes to go, according to the map and cue cards. The breeze felt good. It blew drops of sweat back across Lucy's cheek like wind blowing raindrops to the sides of a windshield. After fifteen minutes they came to the Wrigley Gardens, where everyone received little flags for the front of each bike.

As the whole crowd rode along, Lucy looked around. Jenny and her stepbrother waved; Lucy and Claudette waved back. Erica blew on a whistle as she stopped, and everyone laughed.

I really belong here, Lucy thought for the very first time. Even Julie was glad Lucy had come.

Serena and Roberto rode side by side with Claudette

and Lucy. Soon they came to the finish line. Serena passed a piece of gum to Lucy while they still pedaled, and she snatched it and laughed. When Serena passed another stick, Lucy stuck it into her back pocket.

"Claudette—there's some gum for you in my back pocket!"

She felt Claudette ease it out. "Thanks, Lucy!"

The rally route was lined with balloons at the end, rainbows of them tied to the fences. They looked so pretty, like heads nodding yes and no, up and down, back and forth in the air.

"I love balloons," Lucy said when they stopped.

Serena nodded. "We each get one, if you want." Serena went to the fence and untied two balloons. Then she walked back to Lucy. "Here, you can have mine."

"No, *you* keep it," Lucy said.

"Nope. You love them. You share something much more important—Venus—with me. I want you to have it."

Lucy took both balloons in her hand. "Thanks."

Claudette ran to the fence and took down a balloon. "Take mine, too."

Most of their friends were getting another drink of water, and then they wandered back to where Lucy and Serena had parked their bikes. "What's that?" Erica pointed to Lucy's balloon bouquet.

"Lucy loves balloons," Serena answered for her. "So Claudette and I gave her ours, too."

Erica and Amy went to the fence, too. "Here, take ours. Then you'll have a bigger bouquet. And we're so glad you made a way to come, even though you don't have a sister or brother. Really cool."

Roberto gave his to Lucy, too. "They all say OutSpoken on them," he said. "I've got enough OutSpoken gear."

For some reason all of this made Lucy feel like crying. "Thanks, you guys. Really, really, thanks." Her hand held tight to the balloon strings. Ten-gallon love leaped out of her one-gallon heart.

Mr. Kingsley came down the hill in his golf cart. "I'm going home to set up a little buffet. Lucy's parents are coming, too, after they take down the water bottle booth, and of course Mrs. Chin, who is with Mom and Chantal. Why don't you ride home and change, Lucy, and then meet us at our house? If you can ride the bike yourself, Claudette can come in the cart with me."

Oh. So everyone would already be at Claudette's house before Lucy got a chance to talk with Mrs. Chin? Not if Lucy hurried. Maybe she could make it there before the others.

"All right," Lucy said. "I'll be there, like, really fast."

Mr. Kingsley nodded, and then he and Claudette rode off.

"What's the matter?" Serena must have noticed Lucy's face.

Lucy couldn't tell her without explaining the whole SOS, and it just wasn't finished yet. She hadn't had the dinner or given the packet. And she hoped she'd have good news to share—later.

Instead, she just said, "Can you come over after dinner

tonight? We can read the old diary, write in ours, and tell our SOS. Did you do one?"

"Oh yes," Serena laughed. "I'll see you then."

Lucy and Fireball raced home, her balloon bouquet streaming behind them. She looked on the step—no packet from Mrs. Chin yet.

Lucy ran in, washed the sweat off of her face, and put on some fresh clothes. After putting Venus into the backyard with some fresh water and a rawhide chew, she headed over to Claudette's house.

When she got to the curb, she saw two golf carts—the Kingsleys' and her parents'. They were already there.

Lucy knocked on the door. Claudette let her in. "I'm glad you're here," she said. "I'm starving."

Lucy walked into the dining room. A sandwich buffet was already set out on the table. Her parents were joking, and no one seemed upset. Her mom and dad didn't pull her aside as soon as she walked in the door. *So far, so good.*

Mr. Kingsley prayed, and Chantal munched on barbecue potato chips.

"Her new love," Claudette said about the chips, holding the baby comfortably on one hip.

After they all sat down, Mrs. Chin told them a bit about adoption. "Chantal here is doing just great. I'm sure she's got a wonderful life ahead of her with you guys. There are *so* many more kids who need good homes, though."

Lucy drank in Mrs. Chin's words.

"Older kids, even. Many of them are orphans and need new homes."

Then it happened.

"Lucy," her mother said, "would you please pass those pickles?"

Lucy grabbed the pickle container and handed it to her mother. *Oh no!*

Mrs. Chin looked right at her. "Lucy?" she said.

"I'm very sorry," Mrs. Kingsley said. "How rude of me. I didn't introduce you to Lucy as she came in; we were in such a rush to eat. Mrs. Miriam Chin, this is Lucy Larson, Nathan and Victoria's daughter." She waved toward Lucy's parents. "At least I remembered to introduce you to the Larsons at the booth!"

Mrs. Chin still stared at Lucy. "Lucy Larson. Lucy Larson."

"Pleased to meet you," Lucy said. She looked at Mrs. Chin with pleading eyes.

"Nice to meet you, too, Lucy." Then Mrs. Chin picked up her sandwich and took a bite.

Nothing more was said.

After lunch Lucy and her parents golf-carted home. Dad dropped them off, then went to his office.

"I've got just a few touches to make on my painting, and then you and I can do something fun together, okay?"

Lucy nodded. "I think Venus and I will wait out front and play and train." *And hope that Mrs. Chin still comes by. What if she decides not to give us the package, knowing I'm a girl and not my mother?*

Lucy brushed Venus. Venus kept trying to grab the brush in her mouth. "Hey, give that back, you crazy dog!" Lucy took the brush back, and Venus snatched it away again.

"If I didn't know better, I'd say you were laughing, girl." Venus barked once and then settled down to be brushed.

Half an hour passed. Mom would be done soon.

Lucy and Venus practiced "Sit" and "Stay." Lucy practiced walking up and down the block, getting Venus used to heeling. She continued looking for Mrs. Chin, of course.

An hour later Mom was still painting. And Mr. Kingsley's cart came down the road.

It stopped in front of Lucy's house, and Mrs. Chin got out. By the puzzled look on Mr. Kingsley's face, Lucy could tell that he didn't know why they were stopping there. But of course Lucy knew.

"Sit," Lucy said. Venus, bless her heart, sat down obediently.

"Thanks, girl," Lucy whispered.

Mrs. Chin met Lucy on the porch. "May I pet your dog?"

Anyone who likes dogs is okay in my book, Lucy thought. "Sure!"

After a minute Mrs. Chin handed over a large manila envelope. "Here's the packet of adoption information."

"Mrs. Chin? I just want you to know that I didn't mean for you to think I was my mother. I just wanted to get all of the information to them and talk with them together. Is . . . is that okay?"

Mrs. Chin nodded. "Misunderstandings happen. But the next time I hear from the Larsons, it will have to be from a parent. Okay?"

Lucy nodded. "Deal." She held out her hand to shake.

Mrs. Chin shook her hand and grinned. "Mr. Kingsley is waiting to get me to the ferry, so I'd better go. I've enjoyed meeting you, and I hope we talk again."

"Me too," Lucy said. Boy, wasn't that the truth.

Lucy took the package upstairs to her room and looked it over. It held pictures of babies, toddlers, and even older kids, as Mrs. Chin had said. Lucy stared at their faces and tried to imagine one of them living with her family.

Maybe.

She read over the packet and thought of ways she could help her parents around the house.

Then Lucy made the spaghetti and heated up the meatballs in the microwave. She set the table and even brought down the jar of daisies her mother had put in her room. She set them on the table.

When everything was ready, she called Mom and Dad in, and when they were seated, she brought out the dinner. Dad whistled.

Mom said, "This is just lovely! Especially after you just rode the One Plus One."

"Oh, Mom! That wasn't work; that was fun!"

They talked a bit about the One Plus One, and Lucy told them about her balloon bouquet.

"God really answered your prayers for a rider, didn't He?" her mom said.

Lucy nodded. "And your prayers about finishing your work, right?"

Mom smiled. "Right!"

After they finished chatting about other things and eating, Lucy cleared the table and brought out the brownies.

"I'll make the coffee!" Mom jumped up to take care of it before Lucy could. When it was done, Lucy cleared her throat.

"I have something I want to talk about with you two." She set the packet on the table and explained how she had received it. "I wanted to tell you at just the right time, when we weren't stressed and could plan it out. You said if stuff was planned right, it all worked out in the end," she told her mom. Mom nodded and smiled.

"Anyway, I've been thinking. You guys think Chantal is great, don't you?"

"Yes, we do," Dad said. "And we're very happy for the Kingsleys. But honestly, Lucy, this isn't something we've thought about for ourselves."

"I know," Lucy said. "Me neither, before this week. But it might work. You guys are great parents, and I would like a sister or a brother. And it can't hurt to just investigate it. Right?"

She looked at them, trying to read their faces.

"Chantal is cute," her mother said, softening. "She's spunky, like you were as a baby. I do feel like I know what I'm doing as a mother more now. But children take time, Lucy. I'd have to evaluate if we have that time."

"And the love and patience they'd need," Dad added. "The lifelong commitment to doing what is best for the child, no matter what. Asking a new person into our family isn't like getting a pet."

Lucy nodded. It was true. No one said anything, but her dad did grin when he saw the little faces in the brochure.

"I'll tell you what," he said. "Why don't we pray about it as a family? When we get back to Seattle at the end of the summer, we can look over our commitments, talk about it as a family, and see what we feel after prayer."

That seemed right. After all, Lucy knew the Kingsleys had prayed for months before contacting Mrs. Chin.

"Okay," Lucy agreed. Mom agreed, too, though she held on to the brochure a bit tighter and looked it over again, smiling.

"If we feel, as a family and after prayer and thought, that it should just be us three, will that be okay?"

Lucy thought about the week. Chantal was so cute. But . . . she cried a lot, too. It would be so fun to have a sister to share things with. Maybe even an older one, like Mrs. Chin said! But it was also sad that Claudette didn't have much free time now. And Lucy kind of liked her time with Mom and Dad.

"Yes," Lucy said. "I can see it either way."

"God will let us know," Mom said. "Speaking of which—what gave you the idea to email Mrs. Chin, anyway?"

Lucy explained about the SOS Diary Deed.

"What was Serena's SOS?" Mom asked.

"I don't know!" Lucy said. "And I can't wait to find out! She'll be here in a few minutes, so I'll ask her."

Dad put the adoption packet away, and Lucy went to help her mom pack up her brushes.

"Hey, Lucy! Serena's here," Dad called into the living room. Lucy went to meet her, and they raced upstairs.

"First, the diary." Serena pulled it out of her bag. They opened it up and read.

"Dear Diary," the blocky letters began.

"We did snoop about a bit and found out about the SOS. It was a real disaster, Diary. The first we'd ever seen!"

Serena handed the diary to Lucy, who read Mary's curly writing.

"Someone had to abandon ship, and the family just made it onto a lifeboat. They survived by licking dew off of the boat. Finally the Coast Guard got to them. I'm hoping to interview them for the local paper. Serena says she'll tag along and draw a sketch."

"Wow!" Lucy said to her best friend. "Your great-grandmother liked to draw, just like you!"

"I never knew it," Serena said, awed. "It's very cool."

"Anyway, it's been fun, and I think I can get an interview. In fact, we're on our way now, Diary. If I do, I'll tear it out of the paper and put it in back. See you soon. Ta-ta!"

Lucy took out the envelope from the back of the diary.

Inside were treasures—an old napkin, a tiny horse. And a newspaper clipping all about the rescue. Lucy read it out loud, and then they put it back.

"I'd love to write for a newspaper," Lucy said. "Dreamy. And she actually did it way back then."

The two of them took out their own diary and wrote down their adventures of the week.

"So what was your SOS?" Lucy said.

Serena gigged. "I called for *real* help. I had them send over my sheepskin seat. Get it? Send Over Sheepskin? SOS!"

Lucy laughed. "You goof!"

"And what was yours?"

Lucy explained all about Mrs. Chin and the dinner that night. "Mine was Send Over Sister. SOS!"

They giggled together. Then Serena grew serious.

"If you don't get a sister or brother, will you be devastated?"

Lucy sat still. She looked around her room, then at Venus, sitting by their feet. "No, I mean, I'd love to have a little cute-juice sister. Or even an older brother or sister, you know, to always have. Like you do. But I can be okay with things this way, too. Like the Bible says, God placed me in *this* family."

"Yeah."

"I have what I need. Someone to ride with this week. My dog. My mom and dad. My piano. A best friend." She smiled at the balloons everyone had gathered for her, which now made a bright bouquet in the corner of her room. "And other friends so I'm not always lonely."

"Right!"

"And when I *am* really lonely, God is always there. Everyone is lonely sometimes. Hey! I just figured something out!" She looked at the name on the balloons. "One Plus One can always be God plus me. No matter what."

Serena smiled. "Yep. And for this summer, it can be me plus you, too. Best buddies."

"And Faithful Friends." Lucy took her mother's sketch of the three of them—and Venus—off of the mirror over her dresser and slipped it into the diary before closing it.

"Speaking of One Plus One," Serena said, "I have something for us both to do."

Lucy followed Serena downstairs and outside. Serena's tandem sat on the sidewalk.

"We didn't get to ride together. Want to?"

"Of course! Let's go."

They slipped on the earphones and mouthpieces. Serena got on the front and Lucy on the back, and together they rode down the street into the sweet evening, tandem-talking all the way.

And my God shall supply all your needs according to His riches in glory in Christ Jesus.

PHILIPPIANS 4:19

SANDRA BYRD grew up with a terrific brother, though her little sister wasn't born till Sandra was Lucy's age. Her baby sister used to pull her hair and cry, just like Chantal. But like Chantal, Sandra's sister was also cute and fun.

Sandra lives near beautiful Seattle, between snow-capped Mount Rainier and the Space Needle, with her husband and two children (and let's not forget her new puppy, Duchess). When she's not writing, she's usually reading, but she also likes to scrapbook, listen to music, and spend time with friends. Besides writing THE HIDDEN DIARY books, she's also the author of the bestselling series SECRET SISTERS.

For more information on THE HIDDEN DIARY series, visit Sandra's Web site: *www.sandrabyrd.com*. Or you can write to Sandra at

Sandra Byrd
P.O. Box 1207
Maple Valley, WA 98038

Contents

W9-BNT-900

Chapter 1

KING OF
THE PLANETS

More than two thousand years ago in ancient Rome, people looked into the sky at night. They wanted to understand the universe. They saw lights shining in the darkness. These lights were stars and planets. One light looked bigger and brighter than the others.

Jupiter looks like a bright light in the night sky.

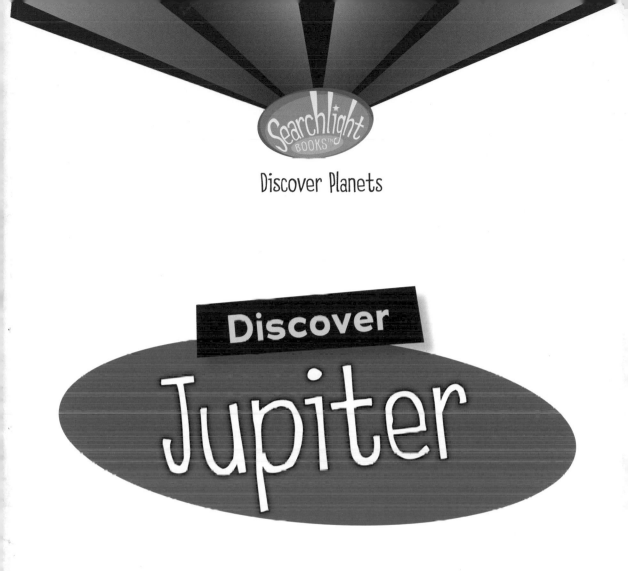

Searchlight BOOKS™

Discover Planets

Discover

Jupiter

Margaret J. Goldstein

Lerner Publications ◆ Minneapolis

Lerner Publications Company
A division of Lerner Publishing Group, Inc.
241 First Avenue North
Minneapolis, MN 55401 USA

For reading levels and more information, look up this title
at www.lernerbooks.com.

Main body text set in Adrianna Regular 14/20.
Typeface provided by Chank.

Library of Congress Cataloging-in-Publication Data

Names: Goldstein, Margaret J., author.
Title: Discover Jupiter / Margaret J. Goldstein.
Description: Minneapolis : Lerner Publications, [2018] | Series: Searchlight books.
    Discover planets | Audience: Ages 8-11. | Audience: Grades 4 to 6. | Includes
    bibliographical references and index.
Identifiers: LCCN 2017046681 (print) | LCCN 2017051672
    (ebook) | ISBN 9781541525429 (eb pdf) | ISBN 9781541523357 (lb : alk. paper) |
    ISBN 9781541527850 (pb : alk. paper)
Subjects: LCSH: Jupiter (Planet)—Juvenile literature. | Space sciences—Juvenile literature.
Classification: LCC QB661 (ebook) | LCC QB661 .G655 2018 (print) | DDC 523.45—dc23

LC record available at https://lccn.loc.gov/2017046681

Manufactured in the United States of America
1-44408-34667-1/12/2018

Jupiter is about 88,846 miles (142,984 km) across at its widest point. Earth is about 7,926 miles (12,756 km) across.

The Romans named it after the king of their gods, Jupiter. Jupiter was the god of light and the sky.

Jupiter is the largest planet in our solar system. It is bigger than all the other planets combined. Jupiter is so big that thirteen hundred Earths could fit inside it!

Hangers-On

A moon is a large object that orbits a planet. Four big moons orbit Jupiter. They are called Ganymede, Callisto, Io, and Europa. Many smaller moons also orbit the planet. Scientists have counted more than sixty of them.

Rings orbit Jupiter too. These rings are flat disks made of dust and tiny pieces of rock. They are thin and hard to see. Small moons sit between Jupiter's rings. These moons and rings travel around Jupiter.

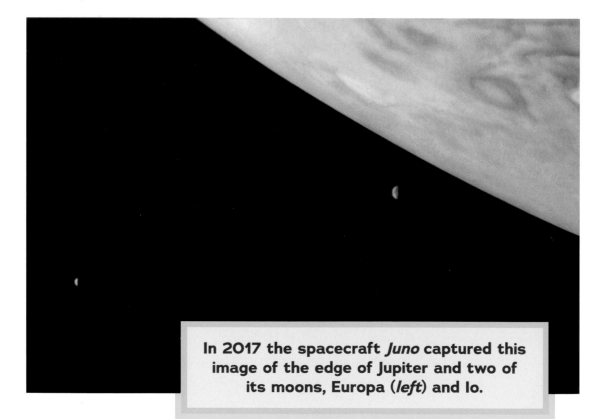

In 2017 the spacecraft *Juno* captured this image of the edge of Jupiter and two of its moons, Europa (*left*) and Io.

STEM Highlight

The spacecraft *Voyager 1* and *Voyager 2* studied Jupiter's largest moons in 1979. Scientists learned a lot about the moons from these spacecraft.

Io has many volcanoes. Callisto is pitted with craters. Europa is covered with a thick crust of ice. Scientists think a deep ocean lies beneath the ice.

Ganymede is the largest moon in our solar system. It is bigger than Mercury, the smallest planet. In 1995 the spacecraft *Galileo* visited Ganymede and found a magnetic field around the moon. Ganymede is the only moon scientist know of that has its own magnetic field.

In this image taken by *Galileo*, the bright spots on the surface of Callisto are craters.

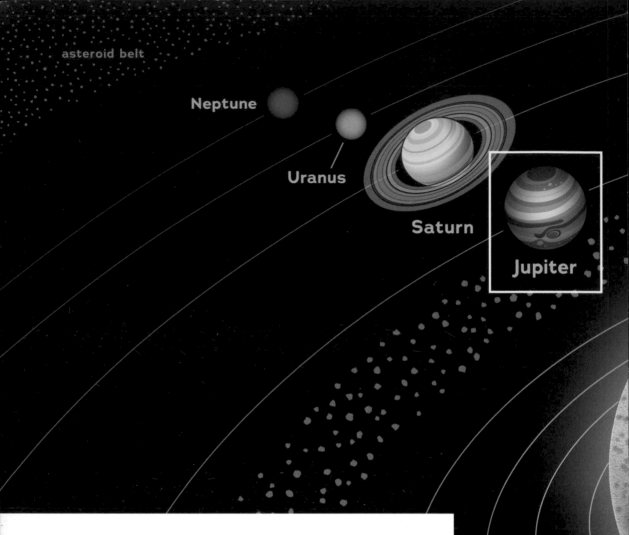

asteroid belt

Neptune

Uranus

Saturn

Jupiter

Our solar system has eight planets. Mercury is the planet closest to the sun. The next closest is Venus, and then come Earth, Mars, Jupiter, Saturn, Uranus, and Neptune.

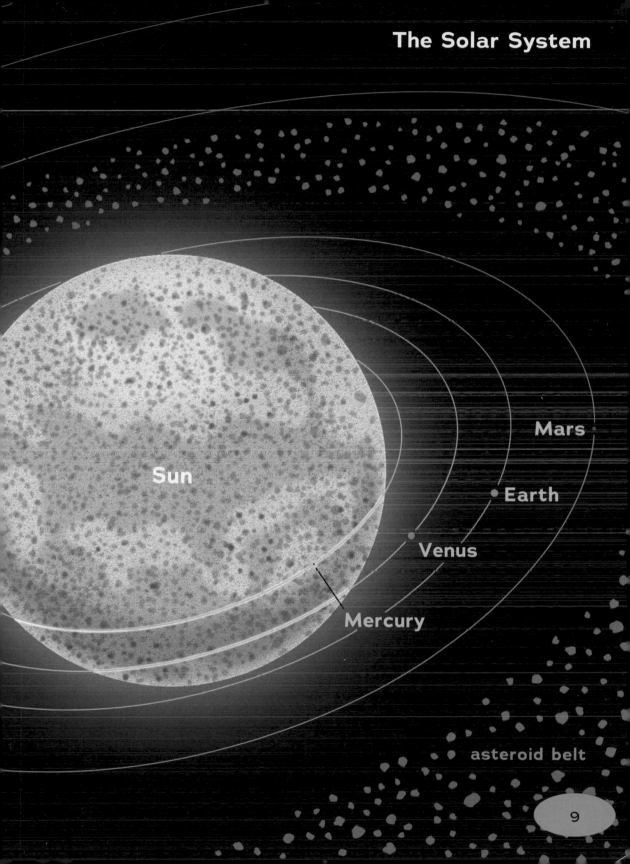

The Solar System

Sun

Mercury

Venus

Earth

Mars

asteroid belt

As Jupiter spins, part of the planet faces away from the sun. This part of the planet is very dark.

On the Move

All the planets in our solar system orbit the sun. A year is the time it takes for a planet to travel once around the sun. One year on Earth takes 365 days. One year on Jupiter takes 11.86 Earth years.

Jupiter spins too. A day is the time it takes for a planet to make one full spin. A day on Earth lasts twenty-four hours. A day on Jupiter lasts nine hours and fifty-five minutes. Jupiter spins faster than any other planet.

Chapter 2

GAS GIANT

If you flew a spacecraft to Jupiter, you'd have nowhere to land. Jupiter doesn't have any solid ground. It doesn't have a rocky surface like Earth. Instead, it is made of gases, including helium and hydrogen. Saturn, Uranus, and Neptune are also big balls of gas. Scientists call these planets gas giants.

Jupiter is made up of gases, just like stars are. Some scientists think that if Jupiter were even bigger, it would be a star instead of a planet.

Stormy Weather

Jupiter's atmosphere is filled with thick, colorful clouds. Light and dark clouds make a striped pattern. The stripes are called zones and belts. Zones are areas of whitish clouds. In zones, winds blow from west to east. Belts are areas of reddish-brown clouds. In belts, winds blow from east to west.

Jupiter is also stormy. Bright bolts of lightning flash through the clouds. Strong winds blow. These winds can reach 400 miles (644 km) per hour.

A powerful telescope took this image of Jupiter, which shows its stormy surface and the zones and belts.

The biggest storm on Jupiter is called the Great Red Spot. It is bigger than Earth. No one knows when the storm began. Many researchers believe British scientist Robert Hooke first saw it through a telescope in 1664. So it might be at least 350 years old.

A camera on the spacecraft *Juno* took this photo of the Great Red Spot in 2017. The photo shows the Great Red Spot's true colors.

STEM Highlight

Comets are icy bodies that travel through a solar system. In 1993 astronomers Eugene and Carolyn Shoemaker and David Levy studied photographs taken with a powerful telescope. The photos showed a comet orbiting Jupiter. Jupiter's powerful gravity had broken it into pieces. The broken comet was headed for a crash with Jupiter.

For six days in July 1994, pieces of the comet hit Jupiter. Scientists on Earth watched. This was the first time they had observed a collision between objects in space. It helped scientists study how other collisions in space have changed the solar system.

A scientist created this image by putting together several photos of the comet hitting Jupiter in 1994. When pieces of the comet hit Jupiter, scientists saw bright flashes of light.

Interior Department

Underneath Jupiter's stormy atmosphere is a thick layer of liquid hydrogen and helium. Beneath that is an even thicker layer of liquid metallic hydrogen. This hot, soupy substance creates Jupiter's magnetic field and electricity. Scientists don't know what the very center of Jupiter is like. It might be a hot ball of rock and metal.

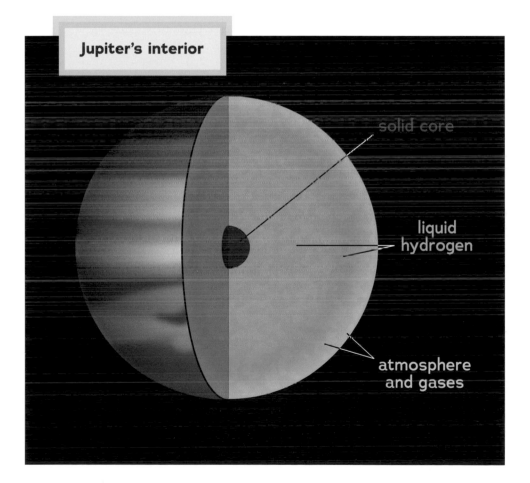

Jupiter's interior

solid core

liquid hydrogen

atmosphere and gases

At the top of its clouds, Jupiter is extremely cold. Temperatures there can be as low as -260°F (-162°C). The deeper you go inside Jupiter, the hotter it becomes. The core might be more than 35,000°F (19,427°C). That's hotter than the surface of the sun!

Chapter 3

LOOKING UP

Ancient sky watchers didn't have telescopes. With just their eyes, they saw Mercury, Venus, Mars, Jupiter, and Saturn at night. They didn't see Neptune or Uranus. These planets are too far away.

Jupiter (*left*) and Venus are the two brightest planets that we can see in the night sky.

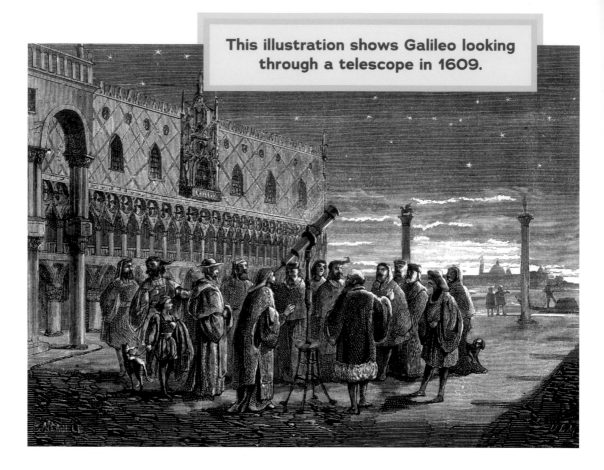

This illustration shows Galileo looking through a telescope in 1609.

With the naked eye, Jupiter looks like a small golden light at night. But with a telescope, you can see the planet's striped atmosphere, its big moons, and the Great Red Spot. In 1610 the telescope was a brand-new invention. That year Italian astronomer Galileo Galilei looked at Jupiter with a telescope. He saw its four biggest moons: Io, Europa, Ganymede, and Callisto. He watched them each night for a week. He saw that they orbited Jupiter.

Eyes on the Sky

After Galileo, other astronomers watched Jupiter through their telescopes. In the late seventeenth century, Italian astronomer Giovanni Cassini studied Jupiter's moons, clouds, and the Great Red Spot. He recorded their movements. By studying these movements, he was able to estimate how quickly the planet was spinning.

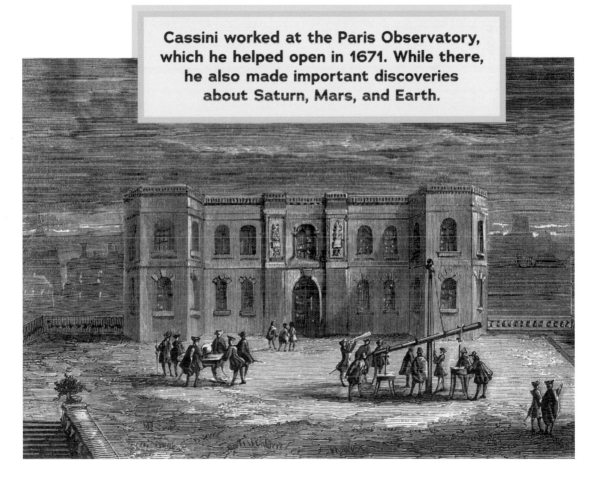

Cassini worked at the Paris Observatory, which he helped open in 1671. While there, he also made important discoveries about Saturn, Mars, and Earth.

The first radio telescopes were built in the 1930s. Scientists used this radio telescope to measure radiation from the sun.

In the twentieth century, engineers built bigger, more powerful telescopes. They also built radio telescopes. These devices detect waves of energy called radiation. Using a radio telescope in 1955, US astronomers Kenneth Franklin and Bernard Burke detected radiation coming from Jupiter. The planet's magnetic field produced the radiation.

STEM Highlight

Auroras are displays of colored light that are visible in the nighttime sky. Auroras occur on Earth near the North Pole and South Pole. The light comes from electrically charged particles moving along Earth's magnetic field and colliding with other particles in Earth's atmosphere.

Auroras take place on Jupiter too (*pictured*). They are much bigger and brighter than auroras on Earth. This may be because of the strength of Jupiter's magnetic field and the speed that the planet spins.

Blast Off

Many space vehicles have visited Jupiter. The vehicles have sent photographs and information back to scientists on Earth.

The spacecraft *Pioneer 10* flew past Jupiter on December 3, 1973. *Pioneer 11* flew past on December 2, 1974. The two spacecraft carried cameras. They carried telescopes and instruments that measured light and radiation. As they flew by Jupiter, they gathered data about its atmosphere and magnetic field.

An artist created this image of *Pioneer 10* flying over Jupiter.

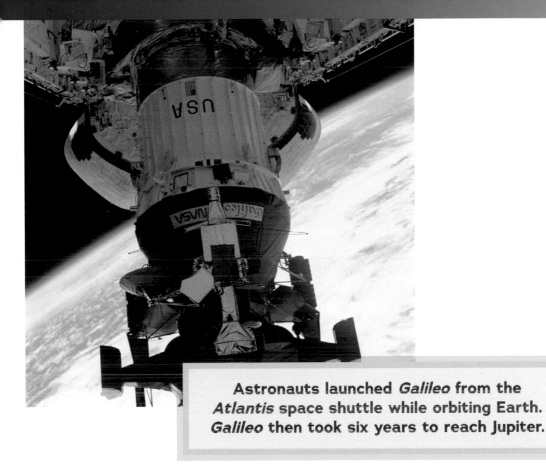

Astronauts launched *Galileo* from the *Atlantis* space shuttle while orbiting Earth. *Galileo* then took six years to reach Jupiter.

In 1979 *Voyagers 1* and *2* made close-up investigations of Jupiter's moons. They photographed the Great Red Spot. They also discovered Jupiter's rings.

The *Galileo* spacecraft reached Jupiter in 1995. One section of *Galileo* left the main craft and dove down through Jupiter's clouds. On the way down, the vehicle analyzed Jupiter's gases and weather systems. *Galileo*'s main craft orbited Jupiter for eight years. The craft studied Io's volcanoes, found Ganymede's magnetic field, and found evidence of a water ocean on Europa.

Chapter 4

MISSION TO JUPITER

A spacecraft called *Juno* left Earth in August 2011 and arrived at Jupiter in July 2016. Then it began to orbit the planet. *Juno* carried eight instruments for studying the planet. These instruments measured light and radiation coming from Jupiter. They also studied Jupiter's gravity and magnetic field.

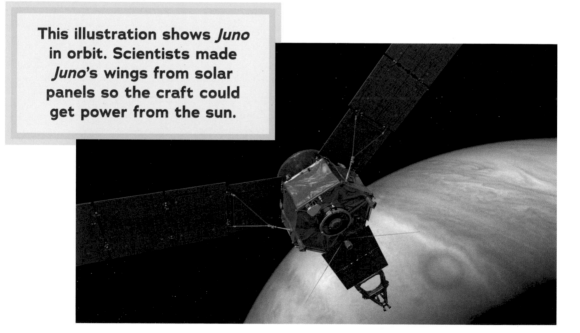

This illustration shows *Juno* in orbit. Scientists made *Juno*'s wings from solar panels so the craft could get power from the sun.

This image was taken by JunoCam. The colors were changed to make Jupiter's stripes easier to see.

A camera called JunoCam took close-up pictures of the Great Red Spot and other parts of Jupiter. It took the first pictures of the north and south poles of the planet. The US National Aeronautics and Space Administration (NASA), which runs the US space program, let people on Earth take part in JunoCam's mission. People could help decide which parts of Jupiter the camera photographed. When the pictures came back to Earth, people could view and make changes to the photos using their own computers.

Discovery

In its first year orbiting Jupiter, *Juno* made exciting discoveries. It found clusters of cyclones at Jupiter's north and south poles. The giant spinning storms are hundreds of miles across.

Juno even recorded whooshing noises coming from Jupiter's auroras. The sounds are too high-pitched for human ears. Machines lowered the pitch so humans could hear them. The sounds come from waves of radiation. By studying them, scientists will learn more about Jupiter's auroras.

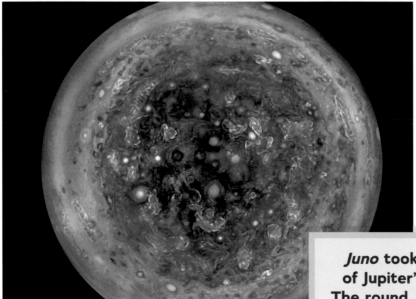

Juno took this picture of Jupiter's south pole. The round, blue shapes in the middle are cyclones.

**An artist's image shows *Juno*
flying over Jupiter's north pole.**

Mission Accomplished

Scientists planned for *Juno* to orbit Jupiter twelve times.
Then, at the end of the mission, they planned to send
Juno to burn up in Jupiter's atmosphere. This way, the
spacecraft wouldn't crash into Jupiter's moons and cause
damage. Thanks to *Juno*, scientists know more than ever
about Jupiter. But there is still much more to find out!

STEM Highlight

Scientists think that life depends on three ingredients: liquid water, elements such as carbon and hydrogen, and energy. All three together can cause chemical reactions that form life. The ocean water on Europa (*pictured*) might be suited for life. The elements might be in the rocky ground beneath the ocean. And volcanoes and hot water might provide the energy to start chemical reactions. NASA plans to send a spacecraft called *Europa Clipper* in the 2020s to study whether life has already formed on Europa.

Looking Ahead

Jupiter is still full of unanswered questions. Scientists are working to find out more about the planet. Here are just a few of Jupiter's mysteries. Maybe one day you'll be the one to solve them!

- Is there life in the ocean on Europa? What will *Europa Clipper* find when it reaches Jupiter's big moon?

- How old is the Great Red Spot? It has been spinning for hundreds of years. Could it be even older? Pictures from JunoCam might tell us more about the big storm.

- Jupiter's auroras are about one hundred times brighter than auroras on Earth. What makes them so bright? Data from *Juno* might solve the mystery.

Glossary

astronomer: a person who studies objects and forces outside Earth's atmosphere, such as planets, stars, and energy traveling through space

atmosphere: a layer of gases surrounding a planet, a moon, or another object in space

aurora: a display of colored lights in the nighttime sky. Auroras appear when electrically charged particles hit a magnetic field.

estimate: to give or form a general idea about something

gravity: a force that pulls objects in space toward one another. Jupiter's gravity pulls objects toward the planet.

magnetic field: a region around a planet or another object that gives off a force called magnetism. Magnetism pulls on some kinds of metal.

orbit: to travel around another object in an oval or circular path

radiation: energy that takes the form of waves or particles

solar system: a group consisting of a star and the planets and other objects that orbit the star. In our solar system, the star is called the sun.

telescope: an instrument that makes distant objects look bigger

volcano: an opening in the surface of a planet or moon through which hot rock, metal, or gases sometimes gush out

Learn More about Jupiter

Books

Chiger, Arielle, and Matthew Elkin. *20 Fun Facts about Gas Giants*. New York: Gareth Stevens, 2015. Take a trip to the outer solar system to explore the gas giants: Jupiter, Saturn, Uranus, and Neptune. This book will be your guide.

Squire, Ann O. *Planet Jupiter*. New York: Children's Press, 2014. Find out more about how Jupiter was discovered and what scientists know about the planet.

Zuchora-Walske, Christine. *We're the Center of the Universe! Science's Biggest Mistakes about Astronomy and Physics*. Minneapolis: Lerner Publications, 2015. In ancient times, astronomers thought everything in the universe circled around Earth. That turned out to be wrong. This book examines changing scientific beliefs.

Websites

Our Universe
https://www.esa.int/esaKIDSen/OurUniverse.html
The European Space Agency hosts this website, which includes sections on the sun, planets and moons, stars and galaxies, comets and meteors, and the entire universe.

Solar System 101
https://solarsystem.nasa.gov/kids/index.cfm
This NASA website lets you explore the sun, planets, moons, and other objects in our solar system. The site also includes games, puzzles, and other activities.

What Is a Planet?
http://kids.nationalgeographic.com/explore/space/what-is-a -planet/#planetary-lineup.jpg
This site from *National Geographic Kids* includes fun facts and pictures, with information about each planet and much more.

Index

Photo Acknowledgments

The images in this book are used with the permission of: Cooldyx/Shutterstock.com, p. 4; NASA/JPL, pp. 5, 7, 14, 16, 22, 23, 25; NASA/JPL-Caltech/SwRI/MSSS/Roman Tkachenko, p. 6; © Laura Westlund/Independent Picture Service, pp. 8–9, 15; NASA/JPL-Caltech/SwRI/MSSS/ Gerald Eichstadt/Sean Doran, p. 10; NASA/JPL-Caltech/SwRI/MSSS/Gerald Eichstaedt/John Rogers, p. 11; NASA/ESA/A. Simon (GSFC), p. 12; NASA/JPL-Caltech/SwRI/MSSS/Bjorn Jonsson, p. 13; Viktar Malyshchyts/Shutterstock.com, p. 17; Universal History Archive/Getty Images, p. 18; Oxford Science Archive/Print Collector/Getty Images, p. 19; Underwood Archives/Getty Images, p. 20; NASA/ESA/J. Nichols (University of Leicester), p. 21; NASA/JPL-Caltech, pp. 24, 27; NASA/ JPL-Caltech/SwRI/MSSS/Betsy Asher Hall/Gervasio Robles, p. 26; NASA/JPL-Caltech/SETI Institute, p. 28.

Front cover: NASA/JPL-Caltech/SwRI/MSSS/Gerald Eichstadt/Sean Doran.